The Last Burp of Mac McGerp

To Rick and Victoria

Text copyright © 2003 by Pam Smallcomb
Illustrations copyright © 2003 by Lizzy Bromley

Type set in Berkeley Oldstyle
The art was done in graphite pencil

Published by Bloomsbury, New York and London
Distributed to the trade by Holtzbrinck Publishers
Library of Congress Cataloging-in-Publication Data:
Smallcomb, Pam, 1954-
The last burp of Mac McGerp / by Pam Smallcomb.   p. cm.
Summary: Mac McGerp, winner of the Best Burper first prize at the Tri-County Fair, and his good friend, Lido, try to figure out how to deal with the new, repressive school principal.
hardcover ISBN 1-58234-856-1 (alk paper)
paperback ISBN 1-58234-868-5
[1. Schools--Fiction. 2. School Principals--Fiction. 3. Belching--Fiction. 4. Best friends--Fiction. 5. Friendship--Fiction.] I. Title.
PZ7.S63914 Las 2003 [Fic]--dc21   2002028344

First U.S. Edition
1 3 5 7 9 10 8 6 4 2

Bloomsbury USA Children's Books
175 Fifth Avenue
New York, NY 10010

Printed in Great Britain

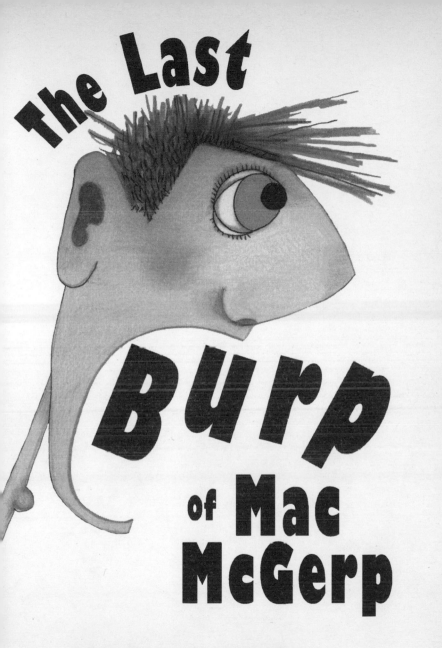

The Last
Burp
of Mac McGerp

PAM SMALLCOMB

Mac McGerp

was the best burper in the whole world. He was only ten years old. He was as skinny as a pencil. But he could suck in air like a vacuum cleaner.

He'd take a big gulp of air and swallow. Then more air. Swallow. And more. Swallow. His Adam's apple would fly up and down. His eyes would start to bug out. His face would turn bright pink and then . . . "ERRRRRRRRRP!!" Out would come a truly magnificent burp.

At first, everyone (except me, of course) thought Mac was really disgusting. But when Mac won first prize at the Tri-County Fair for Best Burper, they changed their minds. Fast. In fact, people started treating him like a hero. Our little town of Withersberg hadn't won anything before. We hadn't even come close. Mac McGerp made Withersberg famous for *something*. We had the best burper in three counties.

After that, Mac burped where, when, and as many times as he wanted to. He'd wave and burp at the old guys hanging out in front of the post office.

He'd burp his order at Fastburger. At school, he'd burp a "hello" to Mrs. Trump, our fifth-grade teacher. He could even burp the entire Pledge of Allegiance.

Mac entered all sorts of competitions. He won big shiny trophies that had his name on them. One said, "Best Interpretation of a Country Western Song, Mac McGerp, First Prize." It was my favorite trophy. It was as tall as me and had a cowboy holding up a giant guitar.

Our town was hoping that Mac would be the next National Burping Champion. That would really put Withersberg on the map. Maybe someday, he could even compete internationally. That would be something. The Burping Olympics. We had high hopes for Mac.

Yeah, Mac's burps were special. He was a genius, really. And he had all kinds of burps. He could belch out a big, wet, dripping, slobbering burp. He could burp like a foghorn, long and low. He could make short, popping burps like a machine gun. But the very best thing about Mac's burps, the thing that made him so special, was that Mac could actually *move* things with his burps.

At first he could only move a milk carton across the lunch table, but by the time he was nine, he could knock a bike over with a burp from ten feet away.

Mac was great, and I should know. I'm Lido Katz, and I'd been Mac's best friend since second grade. But that was all before Mrs. Goodbody came to Walters Elementary School.

Chapter One

Monday: The Day *She* Came

It was the middle of November when Mrs. Goodbody arrived. That Monday started off just like any other. I walked to Mac's house. He was out in his front yard throwing a ball to his dog, Plunger. Mac had on his favorite gray sweatshirt. He practically lived in it. His blond hair stuck out all over his head. Mac always had serious bed head. He didn't care.

We were opposites, Mac and me. He was tall and skinny. Really outgoing and friendly. I was short and not *fat*, but no way was I skinny like Mac. And

I was really shy until I met Mac. I never talked to anyone.

Mac walked up to me that first day in second grade, smiled, and said, "Hey."

"Hi," I said back. I mean, I *had* to talk. I had to *answer* him. Then he asked me if I wanted to play kickball.

"Sure," I said. After that, we always hung out together. I never had a good friend until Mac came. And for some reason, once Mac came to our school, I wasn't as shy as I had been. Well, not around kids anyway. Maybe Mac was contagious, like a cold.

The day Mrs. Goodbody came we had a few minutes until we had to walk up to the school, so we played with Plunger for a while. Then Mac and I started up the street.

We had a regular routine. He'd practice for the Nationals by burping the answers to all my questions. I was kind of like his coach.

"Did you watch *Alien 911* last night?" I remember asking.

"Yeah, the paramedics on Mars were cool," he belched back.

The leaves were falling from the trees. It looked like it was snowing red, orange, and yellow. We raced each other to the steps that led up to the big steel and glass doors of our school.

"I win!" belched Mac.

"Not," I answered.

Mac opened the door and we crammed through to the other side. The school's air washed over us. It smelled like gas heaters and the pine cleaner they used to mop the floor every night. Now and then a freshly shampooed kid would sail by. Sometimes they smelled like coconut, sometimes flowers.

Mac and I hurried to the morning assembly. Mrs. Trump always noticed if you were late. And that's when we met *her*. That's when everything changed for Mac.

Mrs. Trump was on stage with the other teachers. I thought it was strange, all of them lined up like that. Usually they sat with us on the benches. But that day they looked like trained seals, sitting on folding chairs all in a row.

We sat with our fifth-grade class, just like we always did. Morning assembly usually lasted only ten minutes.

I sat next to Mac on one side, and Audrey Troll sat on the other.

"Hi, Mac," she gushed.

"Hey," said Mac.

Audrey Troll was the class brainiac. She got an A on every test she took. And she had a *big* crush on Mac. Audrey and I had been in the same second-grade class when Mac started at Walters. She took one look at him and fell all mushy gushy in love with him. Mac always pretended he didn't notice.

Jarvis Pryor sat on the other side of me. He leaned over.

"Hi, Mac," he said. "How's it going?"

"Hey, Jarvis," said Mac.

"Oh, and hi there, Lido," I said. "How's it going?"

"Okay," I answered myself. "Thanks for asking, Jarvis."

Jarvis laughed. "You're weird, Katz," he said.

The trouble with Jarvis was that *he* wanted to be Mac's best friend. There was only one problem. Mac liked me better. So sometimes Jarvis took it out on me. But most of the time things were cool between us.

Mr. Bertram, one of the sixth-grade teachers, got up and walked across to the microphone.

"Good morning, students," he said. "This morning I have a special surprise for you."

"Great," burped Mac. "The last time there was a 'surprise' we did trash pickup at recess."

Mr. Bertram said, "I have some good news. Today we have a new principal. Her name is Mrs. Goodbody." Mr. Bertram rubbed his hand over his chin like he was checking to see if he had shaved

closely enough. "She's been selected for her special .
. . abilities . . ." His voice trailed off as if he wasn't
sure what to say next. Then he coughed once and
continued. "Her special abilities in discipline and
organization."

He went on to explain that our old principal, Mr.
Stein, had quit last Friday. Right after the food fight
in the cafeteria. I didn't know what he'd gotten so
mad about. We'd eaten most of it off the tables. And
we scraped the rest onto the floor. Some people just
don't have a sense of humor, I guess.

Walters Elementary School had gone through six
principals since I'd been in kindergarten. Six. I guess
we *were* a tough school to get used to. So hearing that
we had a new principal wasn't exactly a surprise.

"Yawn," belched Mac.

"Here we go again," I said.

I stretched my feet out in front of me. Mac did
the same. We settled in for the usual speech from
the new principal about how pleased she was to be
here. Blah, blah, blah. I stared up at the long, thin
glass bulbs that lit the auditorium. I thought about
my baseball card collection. Mac put his head back
and closed his eyes.

Then I heard a sound. I wasn't sure at first what
had made it. Maybe some poor cat had gotten
squished in front of the school. It sort of sounded

like the noise a teakettle makes right before it begins to really scream.

I sat up. Mac sat up. We looked at each other. The sound was coming from in front of us. We slowly looked at the stage. And there she was: Mrs. Goodbody.

She was tall and thin and had on a long, black dress. I mean, I guess it was a dress. It could have been the curtains from a funeral parlor. It covered every part of her except her head. And if you ask me, it should have covered that, too.

She looked like a frozen trout. Her lips were puckered into a tight little circle in front of her teeth. Her gray hair was glued down, slick and shiny against her head.

I looked at Mac. His jaw had dropped wide open. I almost laughed out loud. But then I heard the sound again. It made my teeth hurt to hear it. Well, not my teeth exactly, but the fillings in my back molars.

She was clearing her throat, I guess. She stood in front of the microphone and made the sound three more times. Some kids put their hands up over their ears. Me, I couldn't move. Mac didn't move either.

When she was finished making the noise, she took off her glasses. She reached into a pocket. She pulled out a long, gray piece of cloth. She covered one lens of her glasses and wiped in a circular motion. Around and around and around. She took the cloth and covered the other lens. Around and around and around.

We were hypnotized. Even the kindergartners were quiet. Personally, I think they were scared to death. It wouldn't have surprised me if some of them had been crying.

Mac elbowed me. I looked at him. He had this big, dumb grin on his face.

"No!" I whispered. But it was too late.

Mac was swallowing air. He swallowed and swallowed.

I looked at the stage. Mrs. Goodbody had put her glasses back on. She looked out at all of us. She sucked in air with a hissing sound. And she started to speak.

That's when he did it. Mac let loose with one of his really long burps. It must have lasted fifteen seconds, and I swear it parted the hair of the girl in front of us.

Everyone laughed. Even the kindergartners in the first row stood up and looked back. Their five-year-old faces were red from laughter.

"Good one!" some kid yelled.

The laughter slowly died down. Then an icy chill moved down from the stage, just like when the fog rolls in from the ocean. Mrs. Goodbody stood at that microphone like a statue. A creepy Halloween statue.

She reached up and snatched the microphone. Her white cheeks flashed pink as she began to talk. And her voice. Well, it was all I could do to listen. I felt like the sound of it might actually damage my hearing.

"May I have your attention?!" she yelled. Mrs. Goodbody sucked in a little air after each sentence. Like she was sipping from a glass of water. "I have an announcement to make."

Nobody made a sound. Me, I was hoping that if we were all quiet, she would finish quickly, so that my ears would still work in the sixth grade.

"Ladies and gentlemen," she said. "The party is over."

She ran her tongue slowly over her teeth. She paused for a moment.

"Today is the beginning of a *new* Walters Elementary School," she said. I flinched a little with each word. "As Mr. Bertram said, I have been selected to transform this school into a model of academic excellence." Her trout lips moved up and down as if she had a piece of food caught in her teeth. She took another sip of air.

"In the past, this school has been far too concerned with matters that have nothing to do with improving test scores. Such as teamwork." She gave the teachers a disgusted look. "And creativity." She said "creativity" as if it tasted bad. For a minute I thought she was going to wipe her mouth on her sleeve.

"What matters is RESULTS!" she yelled. I fell off my seat.

"That woman can scream," I whispered as I climbed back up on the bench.

"No duh," Mac whispered back.

Mrs. Goodbody was doing something with her face. She was moving the corners of her mouth. I think she was trying to smile. You know, to try to look a little more friendly. But believe me, it wasn't working.

She smoothed her dress with her hands.

"Now, students," she said sweetly. "I have been hired because I get results. You are the tenth school I have been sent to reform. The other nine schools are now impeccable examples of academics and behavior. The tenth will be no different. I will not allow it to be any other way."

Then her voice got just a little louder. "To meet my goals, I *will* weed out the deadwood at this school. Students and faculty alike. There *will* be discipline and order."

She was starting to shout now. "We *will* improve our test scores! And you *will* follow my rules!" She stopped. She patted back a hair that had fallen onto her forehead. She took a deep breath.

"The first rule is: there will no longer be any football games allowed at recess," she said. "Our liability is too high." A cry went up from all of us. Some dumb kid at the back even dared to "boo" her.

She snapped her head to see where the "boo" had come from. She looked like a bird of prey, scanning for the poor field mouse that had just stuck his head up.

"That is enough," she barked. "Silence!"

I looked at Mac. He looked dazed, like when you're watching a scary movie. You know you should look away because the ax murderer is coming. And the dumb jerk in the movie is just sitting there with his back to the door. You know you should look away, but you just can't.

Mrs. Goodbody scoured the room with her eyes. "Which brings me to the second rule. There will no longer be any burping allowed at this school. How an entire community can support such a vile habit is beyond me. But this is *my* school now. Any student who burps will be sent to see me."

She stared at Mac. I could see Mac tense.

Mrs. Trump had told us all about "fight or flight."

How when we come across something or someone dangerous, our bodies get ready to fight that thing, or run away from it. Well, I was ready for *flight*.

"He will come see me," Mrs. Goodbody said again. "And then he will be suspended. Your parents . . ." she smiled a little as she said this, "will be notified immediately."

She looked away and droned on in her screechy voice about the other rules. I half listened, looking at Mac. He looked at me.

"What are you going to do?" I whispered to him.

"I don't know," Mac whispered back. "I've burped all day whenever I wanted to for the last two years. I mean, come on, I'm in training for the Nationals. I don't know if I *can* stop."

"What about your mom and dad?" I asked. "They'll barbecue you if you get suspended."

Mac's parents were what my mom called a "power couple." Both were lawyers. They were really busy, all the time. I had only met them twice. Once at open house, and once when I went over to Mac's house. The whole time I was there, they were on the phone. They kept telling us to be quiet. So after that, we always went to my house to hang out.

My mom had given up. She was raising me by herself. She was so tired when she got home from work, she usually fell asleep on the couch. As far as my mom was concerned, as long as we didn't break anything or burn the house down, she was happy. She did have one rule: Mac had to go outside to burp.

Mac's parents wanted him to be a straight-A student. They had *big* plans for him. If they had their way, he was going to be a lawyer, too. In seventh grade he was going to a private middle school called St. Anne's. They wanted to be sure Mac didn't screw up their plans.

Mac explained it like this: he was just like a pound puppy. Some people pick out a puppy at the pound because it's so cute and all. But after they get it home they realize they have to feed the puppy. And play with the puppy. And clean up after the puppy.

Well, Mac said his folks would have taken the puppy right back to the pound. Dropped it off and gone out to breakfast. Mac said he was their pound puppy. Only they couldn't take him back.

So when Mac looked up at Mrs. Goodbody that morning, I could tell he was worried.

Then the bell rang. Usually there would have been a stampede to the door. But that day, we were afraid to move. Me, I tried not to breathe too loudly.

Mrs. Goodbody smiled a thin smile that pushed her scrawny cheeks up toward her eyes.

"I'm sure we'll get along just fine," she said. "You may be excused to go to class now. There will be no running. Stay in line and exit one class at a time. First, the kindergarten classes will exit." She pointed a scraggly finger at the kindergartner closest to her. His lower lip trembled.

Poor little guy, I thought.

"You!" she said. "Your row exits first."

We lined up in the hall and waited for Mrs. Trump. There were whispers going up and down the line about Mrs. Goodbody.

By the time we got to our classroom, we all agreed that she was definitely a witch. And she had probably murdered her husband. (*Mrs.* Goodbody? Who or *what* would have married *her*?)

We filed into our room and sat at our desks.

"Class, settle down," Mrs. Trump pleaded. When we were quiet, she took roll. Then she ran her hands through her hair and looked out the window. Mrs. Trump was a good teacher. She was hard enough so that it wasn't boring, but she still had a sense of humor and let us have fun sometimes. I liked her. Mac liked her, too.

She looked out the window and put one hand on her forehead.

"Class," she said, "as you know, I've taught school for twenty-seven years. I've told many of you that I might retire in a couple of years."

She turned and looked at us.

"So I hope you'll understand when I tell you this. I would like those years to be peaceful ones. So our class will follow all of Mrs. Goodbody's rules." She stood up and walked over to Mac.

"Now, Mac," she said as she put her hand on his shoulder, "you've made us all very proud. But from now on, you can't burp anywhere at school. You'll have to practice burping *after* school. Do you understand?"

"Yes, Mrs. Trump," Mac said, being very careful not to burp even one syllable. I knew Mac had to be thinking about the National Burping Competition. If he got suspended, they wouldn't accept his application. And Mac wanted to win that competition badly. The first prize was an all-expenses-paid trip to the Bahamas. Even though Mac's parents wanted him to be a lawyer, Mac had other ideas. Big ones.

Mac and I were going to move to the Bahamas after we got our business degrees in college. It was our dream. It's all we ever talked about. Mac even carried a map folded up in his back pocket. It showed the tip of Florida, and just a little bit to the east and south were all the islands of the Bahamas.

We were going to open the Surf & Burp there. During the day I'd run the surf shop. I'd give lessons and sell my custom-made Lido surfboards. Mac would run the burping competitions at night. It was the perfect plan. Mac wanted to win the Nationals so he could scout the Bahamas for a good location for the Surf & Burp. But that would never happen if he got suspended.

Mrs. Trump took a piece of paper from a folder on her desk and held it up.

"These are the new rules," she said. She turned and wrote them on the chalkboard:

The Ten Rules of
Academic Excellence and Safety

1. no football, kickball, baseball, or soccer
2. no burping or other rude noises
3. no talking in the halls
4. no running at any time
on the school grounds
5. no extracurricular activities
(such as field trips, art, or music)
6. no sitting in groups on the playground
7. no animals or pets in the
classrooms or on campus
8. no classroom parties
9. no more than one
bathroom visit per day
10. no loitering on the school grounds
before or after school

Mrs. Trump turned to the class and smiled. "Okay then. There they are. That's enough of that. Now let's get to work. Let's try to learn something new today. And let's try to have a little fun, too."

"It's against the rules," muttered Mac.

"Yeah," I whispered back. "Rule number eleven: no fun at school."

Mac tried hard. He really did. But he couldn't help it. His first mistake was at lunch.

Mac had been wiggling in his chair for the last ten minutes before the bell. Mrs. Trump kept looking at him. Finally, she said, "Mac, are you feeling all right?"

Mac didn't say anything. He just nodded his head up and down.

The lunch bell rang and Mac was out the door like an Olympic sprinter. I tried to keep up with him, but he was a gray blur speeding down the hall and out the back doors to the playground.

When I got outside I saw a human speck at the very edge of the school property, way out by the fence that bordered Mr. Ellison's farm.

When we were in kindergarten we took a tour of his farm and got really close to the sheep. But everyone at Walters Elementary knew that you were supposed to stay away from the back fence. Mr. Ellison didn't like kids throwing dirt clods at his sheep, or feeding them peanut butter and jelly sandwiches.

I saw that gray dot and knew it was Mac. I looked around. Goodbody was on the playground, but she was busy. She was shrieking at Sean Barry because he had just whacked Lydia Reed on the head with his sack lunch. Lydia was crying because peach yogurt had gotten in her hair. Goodbody wasn't looking my way, so I ran straight for the dot.

As I got closer to Mac, I could see that he had both hands over his mouth.

"Are you okay?" I asked. "If Goodbody sees us back here, she'll burn us at the stake."

Mac pointed to his mouth with one hand while he held the other hand over his mouth.

"You're going to barf?" I asked, taking a few steps back.

He shook his head "No." He picked up a stick and started to write in the dirt. He wrote a *B*. He was turning a funny color of pink. He wrote *U R*.

"No, Mac," I yelled. "Don't do it. She'll hear you!"

Mac started to write the last letter, *P*. But then he flushed a deep red and turned his head toward the fence. Just on the other side, two fat sheep looked back at us. His hands came down from his mouth, and it happened.

Chapter Two

Baa Baa Burp

Mac burped. And it was a powerful one. On any other day I would have been filled with pride to witness a burp like that. It was so strong, it knocked Mac off his feet. He fell onto me, and we both landed on our backsides in the field. At the same time we were flying backward, I looked up to see the two sheep airborne in the other direction.

The sheep flew up and over a feed bin. Luckily, they landed hooves first with a startled, "Baa!"

"Oh, man," Mac groaned. "That one really hurt! But I feel better now."

Then I heard a sound. A shrill whistle. It was Mrs. Goodbody. And she was coming right for us.

Mac turned to me. "Lido, let me do the talking," he said.

"Okay." No argument from me. Mac *was* the better talker.

My mom always said Mac talked like whipped cream tasted: smooth and sweet. But Mac was no angel. He would get into trouble at school for little stuff. Like the 9:45 pencil drop during math. That just about drove Mrs. Trump crazy.

Mac talked us all into dropping our pencils every day at 9:45. First Mrs. Trump yelled at us to try to get us to stop. Then she tried sweet-talking us out of doing it. But for a whole month, Mac had us dropping pencils every day at 9:45. Mac isn't a bad person. When Mrs. Trump's eye started to twitch at 9:40 one day, he gave the signal: two short burps. We knew he was calling it off.

He did other stuff, too. Like somehow he dyed the mashed potatoes at school red. He wouldn't tell me how. He said it would be giving away secrets that had taken him years to learn. Like a magician.

And he told lies. Especially about his homework. I always liked his lies, and when Mrs. Trump would say, "Mac McGerp, where is your homework today, young man?" the whole class would put down their pencils, close their books, and settle in for a nice fat lie.

Each one was different. That's what made it so wonderful. It was like that book *The Arabian Nights*, only Mac had to tell his new tale so Mrs. Trump wouldn't send him to the office. He didn't want to have to explain to his parents about any missing homework. So he lied pretty well.

That day, Mrs. Goodbody came storming up.

"What are you two doing out here?" she said. "You know it's against the rules. And what was that awful noise?"

Mac looked out at the two sheep. They stared back, chewing calmly as though nothing had happened.

"It was them," he said. "I think they have gas."

"Pretty powerful gas," Mrs. Goodbody said. "I could hear it way over there." She pointed to the blacktop. She turned and leaned down to Mac. "You wouldn't be burping, would you, Mr. McGerp?"

"Oh, no," Mac said. "Burping is against the rules." He looked up at her sweetly.

Mrs. Goodbody glared at him. The veins in her neck were throbbing. She looked around to see if anyone could hear her.

"Look, you loathsome little toad," she sneered. "I've broken tougher cookies than you. Simply crumbled them into dust." She ground her fingers into a fist. She opened up her palm and pretended to blow dust out of her hand. "For your information, after reforming your sad little school, I intend to be appointed to the Board of Education. At which point, I will be in an air-conditioned office, miles away from the nearest whining brat. So if you think *you're* going to get in my way, think again."

She stopped. She sipped some air. She ran the fingers of one hand across her mouth. Then she smiled.

I just stood there. I couldn't move. I'd never seen anyone like her. I stared at her mouth while she smiled. Maybe she had sharp, sawlike teeth in the back where I couldn't see them.

Mrs. Goodbody leaned over to Mac. "And what's this I hear?" she hissed into his ear. "That your parents want to send you to St. Anne's?" She tapped his earlobe once with her fingernail. "Guess what? St. Anne's doesn't accept students who have been suspended." She stood up and adjusted the collar of her dress. "So perhaps you should get back to the playground."

Mrs. Goodbody turned and swished back to the blacktop. To his credit, Mac kept smiling until she was gone.

"Whoa, close one," I said. "What *is* she, anyway?"

"I don't know," said Mac. He laughed nervously. "But whatever she is, I don't think she likes me." He thought for a minute. "What am I going to do, Lido? I don't know if I can hold a burp all day. Remember the red potatoes? After that my dad said that if he gets one more phone call from the school, I can't compete anymore."

"But you've got to compete," I said. "The Surf and Burp depends on it. So you just *can't* burp."

Somehow Mac behaved the rest of the day. He didn't burp through reading, English, or social studies. He didn't say a word. He just sat very still.

Right before the 2:30 bell rang, Mrs. Goodbody stormed in. Her eyes locked onto Mac. She turned and smiled at Mrs. Trump. Then she looked around the room at the rest of us. She frowned.

"Class, your posture is appalling," she said. "You look like a bunch of dead jellyfish." Jarvis Pryor snorted. She turned to him and glared. "Sit up straight and be quiet! I have an important announcement to make."

She leaned forward a little. The front row leaned back a little. She started quietly. "As you know, Friday is the Science Fair. The superintendent of schools is attending this event at *my* invitation. This is my . . . I mean, *our* opportunity to show him how much this school has changed. So I want to make something perfectly clear. *Everyone* will bring in a science project. Everyone!" Now she was yelling again.

She paused. She sipped some air. She looked at the fingernails on her left hand. Then she looked at us. "You will set up your exhibits in the auditorium after school."

She stood up straight and turned to Mrs. Trump. "Mrs. Trump, I will need two students to stay with the class exhibits until the parents arrive at six-thirty that night."

I looked at Mrs. Trump. She looked hypnotized, like a deer in the headlights of a truck.

Mrs. Goodbody whipped out a clipboard from behind her back. She clicked the end of her ballpoint pen.

"Mrs. Trump!" she shouted. "I need the names of two of your students."

"Oh, oh yes," Mrs. Trump said as she tore her gaze away from Mrs. Goodbody. I knew how she felt. Had Mrs. Goodbody *always* been this way? I wondered if she had been a scary kid. Maybe she was even a scary baby. *Was* she ever a baby? It didn't seem possible.

"All right, class," Mrs. Trump said as she turned to us. "Let's see a show of hands. Who would like to stay with Mrs. Goodbody after school on Friday and look after our science projects?"

Our arms were glued to our sides. Eyes stared at the tops of desks with utter fascination.

"Class?" She sounded tense. Then she caught my eye. "Lido, what about you? You're such a responsible boy." She turned to Mrs. Goodbody. "Lido always helps me after class."

"Well?" Mrs. Goodbody stared at me as she tapped the edge of her clipboard.

What could I say? I liked Mrs. Trump.

"Sure, Mrs. Trump," I said. "I can do it."

Jarvis Pryor made a little kissing sound in back of me.

"Teacher's pet," he whispered.

"Shut up, Jarvis," whispered Mac.

"And Mac." Mrs. Trump sounded relieved. "You come and help Lido. Lido and Mac will help you, Mrs. Goodbody." Mrs. Trump twirled the end of her scarf nervously.

"Is that so?" Mrs. Goodbody asked. It was the sweet voice again. "The great Mac McGerp is going to take time away from his burping to help with the Science Fair? Well, isn't that . . ." She paused and sipped some air. "Isn't that . . . *special*."

Mac just sat there. I tried to kick the side of his chair to snap him out of it.

"Very well." Mrs. Goodbody scratched our names across the pad of paper on her clipboard.

"Come see me at two o'clock on Friday. We'll go over your responsibilities before the last bell. Then the two of you will go with me to the auditorium." She turned to Mrs. Trump.

"Continue," she said. She turned and walked out the door. Her dress made a crackling sound as it brushed against the desks in the front row. Audrey Troll quickly tucked her legs up before Mrs. Goodbody's dress could touch her.

The door closed. A big sigh went around the room. Mrs. Trump looked exhausted.

"Don't forget your homework packets. And remember to pace yourself. Don't wait to do all your homework on Thursday night." She looked at Mac.

The bell rang. We waited, hands on backpacks, waiting for the two best words of the day.

"Class dismissed."

When Mac and I got out the front door of the school, he burped again. It wasn't as powerful as the sheep burp, but it still knocked a first-grade girl off her feet.

"Sorry," said Mac as he helped her up. "I couldn't hold it in anymore."

"That's okay, Mac," she said as she skipped down the sidewalk.

"Mac," I said. "What are you going to do? You're dangerous when you hold your burps in."

Mac looked at me and smiled. "I think it's time to get to know Mrs. Goodbody."

Uh oh, I thought. Because when Mac smiled like that, it could mean only one thing. Trouble. Big trouble.

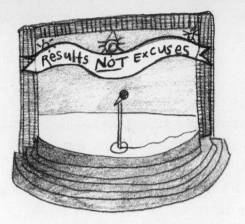

Chapter Three

Tuesday: Behind Every Rule

On Tuesday I stopped by Mac's house on the way to school. His mom said he had left already. I got a bad feeling. Mac was up to something. I just hoped he knew what he was doing.

When I got to morning assembly, a huge red banner was hanging over the stage. RESULTS, NOT EXCUSES! was written in bold black letters across it. I sat down next to Mac.

"Hey," said Mac, looking up from his Bahamas map. "Like the new banner? It's a happy little message, don't you think?"

"Yeah, real happy," I said. "Hey, why did you come to school so early?"

"No reason," said Mac. There was that smile again.

"Don't forget, no burping," I said.

"I think I can make it to two-thirty," said Mac. "But after that, I have to burp. I might explode if I don't."

Jarvis Pryor sat down next to Mac.

"I told my cousin about Goodbody," he said. "She told me something about her. Something bad."

"What?" Mac and I said together.

"Well, Jessie said . . . Jessie, she's my cousin," said Jarvis. "Well, she ain't my real cousin—"

"Jarvis!" said Mac. Sometimes Jarvis took awhile to get to the point. "What did she say about Goodbody?"

"She said," he leaned over to Mac, "that once Goodbody came to their school, kids disappeared. They were there one day, gone the next." Jarvis looked up at the stage. "Nobody knew what happened to them."

Mac and I looked at each other. We looked up at Goodbody.

"You know what else Jessie said?" asked Jarvis. We shook our heads "no." "She said that's why Goodbody always wears black. Out of respect for all the kids she's done in."

"But if she killed them," said Mac, "where are their bodies?"

Jarvis shook his head. "Jessie didn't know. But my other cousin, Ellie, she's my cousin from my great aunt—"

"Jarvis!" I said. "Focus!"

"Oh yeah. Well, Ellie, she goes to Cedar Grove Elementary, and she said when Goodbody was at her school she put them in the cafeteria." Jarvis made a face. He pointed to his mouth. "You know . . ."

Mac and I looked at each other. What was he saying? In the cafeteria? Then I got it. He meant *in* the cafeteria. As in *in* the food.

I wasn't sure if I could ever buy lunch again.

"Attention, please," said Mrs. Trump. "Please stand for the Pledge of Allegiance." She led us in the pledge. Then Mrs. Goodbody walked up the steps to the stage. She sat in the principal's chair next to the podium.

Mrs. Trump reminded everyone that there was roadwork being done in front of the school. Orange safety cones were circling a big hole in the street.

"So be very careful on your bikes and when you cross the street," she said. "Now, Mrs. Goodbody would like to say a few words."

Mrs. Goodbody stood up and walked to the microphone. She sucked air in over her teeth. Mac and I tensed. It was like waiting for someone to rip a Band-Aid off your knee.

"Good morning, students," she said. She was waiting for something. She just kept looking at us.

"Oh, oh yeah, good morning," we finally all muttered back.

"Today we will start my program of order and discipline," she said. "We are going to transform the halls of this school. They will become shining examples. They will show our guests that we are achieving our academic and disciplinary goals." She waved her arm and pointed to the banner. "This will be the motto of Walters Elementary School. Let's read it together."

"Results, not excuses," we muttered.

"I can't hear you!" she screamed.

"Results, not excuses!" we screamed back.

"Much better." She gave us that thin smile again. I felt goose bumps on my arms. "Today each of you will write ten things that you like about this school. We will post these in the hall. The superintendent of schools will be here Friday, so write neatly! I expect *all* our students to have their lists done today." She eyed the teachers.

Mac rolled his eyes. "Oh, brother," he whispered.

"And remember," she continued. "There is no talking allowed in the hallways. It is disruptive to the other students. More important, it is disruptive to me. You may now go to class." She pointed at the same little kindergartner.

The little guy flinched and headed for the door. That's when Mrs. Goodbody turned around to talk to the teachers. And that's when we saw the sign on her backside. It said

RULES FIRST, RULES LAST,
IF YOU DON'T LIKE RULES, YOU
CAN KISS MY BEHIND.

Only it didn't say "behind," it said the other word.

The whole auditorium howled with laughter. Except for that little kindergartner in the front row. He looked too scared to laugh.

"Hey, Mrs. Goodbody!" someone yelled. "You have a sign on your butt!"

I looked over at Mac. He was grinning from ear to ear.

Mrs. Goodbody turned around slowly. Her face was really red. She looked mad enough for her brains to be boiling.

She reached her hand in back of her and ripped

the sign off. She looked down at the words. I could see her lips twitching as she read.

"Whoever," she started, her voice even squeakier than normal. "Whoever did this will be punished. And I *will* find out who you are. Now it is time to go to class." She crumpled the sign in her hand. Then she whipped her head in my direction. I gasped. But she wasn't looking at me. She was looking right at Mac.

"You're dead," I told him.

"Welcome to Walters Elementary, Mrs. Goodbody," Mac said softly.

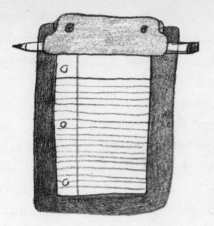

Chapter Four

Goodbody Has to Go

I couldn't talk to Mac in the hall, because Mrs. Goodbody was patrolling. She had her clipboard and was writing down the names of anyone who talked. If you got your name on her list, you missed recess. Not only that, but you had to spend the whole time in the library with *her*. So I kept really quiet.

When we made it into Mrs. Trump's class, we all gasped for air. Then we all started talking at once. Mrs. Trump had to stand on her chair to get our attention.

"Please, class," she shouted. "Take your seats."

We gradually settled down. I still hadn't talked to Mac about the sign. He looked pretty pleased with himself.

"Now, class," Mrs. Trump said, "I have only one thing to say about this morning. It is wrong to embarrass someone like that. I certainly hope that it wasn't one of my students who did that." She glanced at Mac. "Now, we have a lot to do today. Open your journals and list ten things that you like about our school."

It got quiet then, just the noises of pens on paper and the occasional cough or sneeze. Mac looked good, and I thought to myself, *Maybe he won't need to burp.*

But I was wrong. By lunchtime, Mac was looking a little green.

"What's wrong?" I asked.

"It's making me sick," he said.

"What?" I said.

"Swallowing my burps," he said. "It's the only way I can keep from burping. My stomach feels all bloated and squishy inside." He rubbed his stomach. "I don't feel so good."

"Hey," I said. "I know! Why don't you go home sick? That way you can burp all you want and no one will hear you."

"No one's home," Mac said. "My dad's at work. My mom took the day off to see my aunt. If I call my dad and ask him to take me home so I can burp, he'll have a complete cow. Not to mention, he'd miss some stupid meeting."

"Yeah," I said.

"Besides," he said, "that would only work for today. I'd still have to get through tomorrow and the next day." He took a sip of chocolate milk. "No, the only solution is for Goodbody to leave." He smiled and patted me on the shoulder. "And I'm going to help her leave. And guess what? You're going to help me."

"No way, Mac," I stuttered. "She'll destroy me. She'll destroy both of us. Goodbody is so mean she makes Scrooge look like the Easter Bunny."

"Come on, Lido," Mac said. "You don't want to spend the rest of fifth grade and all of sixth grade with Goodbody, do you? Is that any way to live? I don't know about you, but I *like* all the stuff she made rules against. What about your civil liberties? What about freedom?"

The bad thing about being friends with Mac was that he had this kind of power over you. When Mac said something like, "Let's get Mrs. Goodbody to quit," anyone in their right mind would have run the other way. But when Mac talked about two more years of Goodbody rules and no football, no art, no running, and no talking, I kind of agreed with him.

"Listen, Lido, it's like this," Mac said. "Goodbody shouldn't be running a school . . . a prison maybe, but not a school."

"But Mac," I said. "What can we do? She's not like the other principals. . . . She's . . . well, she's pretty scary."

Mac nodded his head in agreement. "Yes she is," he said. "So we'll have to be careful."

"I've got a bad feeling about this," I said.

We walked to the trash cans and dumped the leftovers from our lunch. We slammed the trays down on the tray cart. We were almost through the cafeteria doors when a voice came over the loudspeaker.

"Would Mac McGerp and Lido Katz please report to the office?"

"Oh, man," I said. Mac patted me on the back.

"Just be cool," Mac said. "And Lido, let me do the talking."

"I'm so very, very dead," I said.

Chapter Five

The Bottom of the Food Chain

Mac's color was still a little green when we opened the office door, but he was acting like nothing was wrong.

"Hi, Mrs. Hoover," he said to the secretary. "Did Mrs. Goodbody want to see us about the Science Fair?"

"She wants to see you," she said, opening the door to Mrs. Goodbody's office, "about this morning's assembly. Good luck."

My stomach flipped a small somersault. I'd never been called into the principal's office before. I kept thinking about what my mom would say. It wasn't making my stomach feel any better. I thought about asking Mrs. Hoover if I could go to the nurse's office and lie down, but Mac grabbed my arm and pulled me in. Mrs. Hoover shut the door behind us.

Mrs. Goodbody's back was to us.

Mac put his hand on my shoulder. "Mrs. Goodbody," he said, "Lido had nothing to do with this. I'm not admitting anything, you understand. But I *know* Lido didn't do it." He was using his small voice. The one that sounded like he was trying to squeeze his vocal cords so a burp wouldn't sneak out.

She just stood there looking out the window. On her desk was a small metal cage. Inside was a little white rat. It looked up at us and sniffed the air.

Maybe Goodbody isn't so bad, I thought. *I mean, how bad can she be? She has a pet. A person who likes animals couldn't possibly do what Jarvis's cousins say she did.*

One of her hands rested on the windowsill, and she tapped the glass with a long red fingernail.

Tap. Tap. Tap.

"Uh, Mrs. Goodbody?" I said. Maybe she was a little deaf.

Tap. Tap.

Then she turned, slowly, and looked me right in

the eye. I'd never seen her up close before. Her eyes were gray. The color that the sky looks right before it snows.

"Are you Lido Katz?" she asked.

"Y . . . y . . . yes," I stammered. I felt myself blush.

She stood and stared at me. I looked away. I looked at Mac. Mac had a funny expression on his face. I couldn't tell what it meant.

Somebody should say something, I thought. Maybe Mrs. Goodbody just needed another chance to get to know us. Things *had* gotten off to a bad start. What we needed was to take a deep breath and start over. After all, Mac was a great guy. And I wasn't so bad either. A little nervous now and then, but in general, okay. Maybe I could help the situation. You know, be friendly. Lighten things up a little.

I should have just kept my mouth shut.

"So, Mrs. Goodbody." I tried to sound extra cheerful. "I see you have a pet rat. Guess what? I like animals, too. And Mac here, he has a dog named Plunger."

She glared at me. "That is not a pet, you imbecile. I keep a rat on my desk as a reminder."

"A reminder?" I said. What was she talking about?

"Yes. It reminds me that life is a food chain.

Even *you* know about the food chain, don't you?" she said sarcastically.

"That's the order that things eat other things," I said. I mean, how dumb did she think I was? I looked at Mac and smiled. I could handle this talking-to-the-principal thing. It was going pretty well, I thought. Mac was looking at the rat. He looked kind of worried.

"That's right, my little moron," she said. "Exactly. Wolves eat rabbits. Lions eat zebras. It helps me to see that rat. It reminds me of each one of you putrid students. That rat will be eaten at the end of the week by a very hungry snake I know. There will be a new rat on my desk next Monday."

She took a pencil off her desk and let the rat nibble the end.

"Always remember who is at the top of the food chain. *I* am at the top of the food chain at Walters Elementary School."

I'd rather have the snake, I thought.

Mac's stomach was making weird gurgling noises. He was still staring at the rat.

Suddenly, Mrs. Goodbody slammed her hand down against the top of the cage. The rat sprang into the air and then realized he had nowhere to run. Mrs. Goodbody smiled. The rat tried to hide in a corner.

"Well now, gentlemen," she said. "I think we need to get something straight." She came a step closer. I took a step back.

"I think you need to hear me say something," she said. "Especially you, Mr. McGerp." She got very close to Mac and leaned down. Her face was inches from his.

"I am not going anywhere," she said. "So if that prank of yours is some childish attempt to get me to leave, think again. Believe me, you'll both be gone from Walters Elementary School long before I ever will."

I made a note to myself to apologize to Jarvis for doubting his cousins.

Mac didn't say anything. I waited for him to answer her. But he just stood there. What was wrong with him? It wasn't like Mac to be quiet.

"Um, Mrs. Goodbody?" I said. "May we go now?"

"Yes," she said. "But rest assured, I will think of an appropriate punishment for the two of you." She walked back to the window and looked out over the playground. "Think about what I said." She started tapping the windowpane again.

"Come on, Mac," I said as I jerked his arm.

He came out of his trance and said, "Have a good day, Mrs. Goodbody." His voice sounded hoarse.

Her fingernail stopped its tapping for a beat. Then it began again. Tap. Tap. I grabbed Mac and pushed him out of her office.

"What's the matter with you?" I whispered. "Why didn't you answer her?"

"Gotta burp!" he choked.

Mac and I walked as quickly as we could to the boys' bathroom.

"Flush all the toilets!" Mac squeaked. He looked desperate. "Turn on the water!" Mac ran into one of the stalls and slammed the door shut.

I ran around the bathroom and did what he ordered.

"Okay, Mac," I said. "That's as much background noise as I can give you."

"Get down, Lido!" Mac yelled from inside. I hit the floor. Mac burped. The door to his stall flew off its hinges. It ricocheted back and forth against the bathroom walls a few times. *Zing! Thwack-thwack-thwack-thwack!* Then it slid to the ground, finally coming to a stop in front of me.

"Whoa!" I said as I jumped up. "That was great!" I swear, watching that burp was better than the Fourth of July.

"Let's get out of here," Mac said. "Goodbody will be here in no time."

We opened the bathroom door and peeked out.

Two teachers had already come out of their class-rooms and were looking around for the cause of the noise. Mac and I hurried down the hall to the safety of Mrs. Trump's class.

"Boys," she said as we came in, "where have you been? You know how I feel about being tardy after lunch."

"Uh," Mac said, "we had to go to the office."

Audrey Troll looked at Mac with big goo-goo "I love you" eyes and giggled.

"Oh," Mrs. Trump said, looking worried. "Well, see me after school today and we'll discuss it."

After school, we told Mrs. Trump that Mrs. Goodbody thought we had put the sign on her behind.

"Mac," she said, "did you put that sign on Mrs. Goodbody?"

"I didn't put it on her, Mrs. Trump," Mac said. "I swear."

I told you he was good at lying. I just looked down at my feet.

"Lido?" she said. "Did you?"

I looked up at her. "No way, Mrs. Trump." I was kind of surprised she'd even ask me. And I know it's wrong, but I was kind of proud, too. Mrs. Trump actually thought I was brave enough to do some-thing like that to Mrs. Goodbody. Me. Lido Katz.

"Well then," she said. "I suggest you give Mrs. Goodbody a lot of space. You two don't want your parents getting a phone call."

Mac actually looked sorry. He knew Mrs. Trump liked us.

"Right," he said. "We'll be good. And you know something, Mrs. T? You shouldn't retire. You're the best teacher at this school."

Mrs. Trump smiled and said, "That's a very nice compliment, Mac. And may I say that you and Lido are two of the most *interesting* students I have. There's never a dull day when you two are at school."

"Thanks," I said. Good old Mrs. Trump. Interesting. That was good, right?

"Now," she said, "would you do me a favor on your way out? Would you post these lists the class made on their ten favorite things in the hall display case? Mrs. Goodbody wants them up by tomorrow."

When we got in the hall, I turned to Mac and whispered, "How could you lie to Mrs. Trump? She really likes us."

"I didn't lie." Mac smiled. "I didn't PUT the sign on old Goodbutt. I just put it on her chair. SHE sat on it. I had nothing to do with it getting on her." He hummed as he walked to the display case.

"I guess so," I said. "Still, she wouldn't have had

it on her rear end if you hadn't put it on her chair."

"Listen, Lido," Mac started, but then he stopped. He looked at the display cases that lined the hall. They were all empty, except for the lists from the other classes.

"Hey, where did all the stuff in the cases go?" he said. "Where are my trophies?"

For two years Mac had donated all his best trophies to the school. I watched his jaw tense.

"Take it easy, Mac," I said. "She probably put them in the storeroom."

"She'd better have," he said. He set the lists inside the first case and stormed off toward the janitor's storeroom.

We opened the storeroom door. It smelled like dust and lemon furniture polish. The odor of burnt coffee wafted from the old coffeemaker that sat on top of a filing cabinet in the corner.

Mr. Henkley sat behind a wooden desk. Old rock music blared out of his radio.

"Hey, Mr. Henkley," Mac said. Mr. Henkley had his feet on the desk and his hands clasped in back of his head. His eyes were closed and he had a happy grin on his face.

"Mr. Henkley," Mac said again. Mr. Henkley didn't move. One foot swayed back and forth to the music.

I heard the door open in back of me.

"MR. HENKLEY!" It was *her* voice.

Mr. Henkley sat up so fast he almost fell out of his chair.

"What are you doing?!" she shrieked at him. I ran my tongue over my molars. Her voice reminded me of the time I accidentally chewed the foil on one of those little chocolate Easter eggs.

"Turn that radio off!"

Mr. Henkley tried to turn the radio off, but turned it up instead.

"Sorry, Mrs. Goodbody," he shouted over the noise. "I was just taking a break." He finally just reached down and unplugged it.

"Mr. Henkley." She brought her hands together and touched the tips of her fingers to her chin. "Let's see if I can make myself clear. There are no *breaks* until five P.M. If that is a problem for you, then maybe you should work elsewhere."

Mr. Henkley looked embarrassed. I had never heard anyone talk to him like that before. Mr. Henkley always worked hard. Lots of times he came in on the weekends and did yard work at the school for free. I wished I could think of something to say. Something that would make Mr. Henkley feel better. Or something that would make Mrs. Goodbody shut up. But I probably wouldn't have said it even if

I'd been able to think of it.

Mr. Henkley picked his tool belt up off his desk. "No, Mrs. Goodbody," he said. "That's not a problem." He stood up and walked past Mac and me.

Mrs. Goodbody scowled at us. She looked at Mac like he was a piece of rotting fish.

"What are you doing here? The bell rang fifteen minutes ago. You should be on your way home."

Mac turned and faced her. "Where are they?" he said.

"Where is what?" she said with a sly smile. "Have you lost something?"

"Where are my trophies?" Mac looked like he was going to lose it.

"Trophies?" she said. "Oh, you mean those hideous dust collectors in the display cases? Really, I can't imagine what the school was thinking to put them there."

"Where are they?" Mac said again through clenched teeth.

"They are where they belong," she snapped. "They are in the trash." She turned and swished out of the room, her black dress wiping the walls on her way out.

I couldn't believe it. Mac's trophies were price-less. I mean, how many people do you know who

47

win contests for burping? And *she* had thrown them in the trash.

Mac's hands were clenched by his side.

"Come on," he said, grabbing an empty box by the door.

"Okay," I said. I sure hoped they weren't broken. I switched off the coffeemaker for Mr. Henkley. If Goodbody got that mad at him for taking a break, think of what she would do to him if the coffeemaker burned down the school.

Mac didn't talk on the way to the trash can. When we got there, he moved a smaller can next to the big metal one. He turned it upside down, climbed up, and vaulted over the side.

"Do you see them?" I called.

"Yeah," he said. "They're covered in cafeteria slime."

He handed them over the lip of the can, one by one. I lined them up on the ground. They smelled awful, as if every bad cafeteria smell had been warmed up and spread on Mac's trophies like jam on toast.

"I think that's it," Mac said. He pulled himself up and swung a leg over the edge of the can. He dropped down next to me.

"I'm sorry, Mac," I said. I couldn't think of anything else to say.

"It's okay, Lido," he said. He patted me on the back. "I'll clean them up and they'll be as good as new." He put them in the box and hoisted it up onto his shoulder. "I'll see you later. I've got some thinking to do. Because, you know," he said as he walked off, "this means war."

Mac left, carrying his box of trophies. I could hear him burping "America the Beautiful" on his way.

Chapter Six

Ten Things

"I'll go put the lists up!" I called after him.

By now I was getting a little worried. What did he mean, "war"? Mac had never done anything really bad before, but nobody had ever touched his trophies, much less put them in the Dumpster.

I opened the hall door and looked around for Goodbody. The hall was empty. I hoped she had gone home, but there was a chance that she was still there, maybe in her office.

Whoever designed our school didn't have a lot of imagination. It was just a big rectangle with a hall that cut straight through the center. Classrooms were on each side of the hall, and right in the middle on one side was the principal's office. Unfortunately, I had to go by her office to get to the display cases.

I walked quietly to the middle of the school. Her door was right in front of me. It was open, and I could hear two people talking.

"I want his file, Mrs. Hoover." It was Goodbody. Her voice was icy and angry. "He doesn't want to follow the rules? Well, then he can attend school elsewhere. There are plenty of correctional facilities that will take him."

"But Mrs. Goodbody, he's really a *good* boy. He just has a lot of life in him. He's one of those independent souls. You wait and see; he'll be a leader some day." Good old Mrs. Hoover. She was defending some poor kid.

"Mrs. Hoover." Goodbody's voice pierced the air like a jackhammer. "Bring me Mac McGerp's file."

I couldn't move. Mac was going to get it for sure. Why did she want his file? What was in a file anyway? I pressed against the cool brick wall and listened.

"And while you're at it," Mrs. Goodbody snapped, "bring me the file of his silly little friend. Lido Katz."

Me? What had I done? My mom was going to go

through the roof if I got in trouble with the new principal. Then she would say I couldn't hang around with Mac anymore. This was bad.

"Lido Katz?" Mrs. Hoover said. She chuckled. "Mrs. Goodbody, you don't know him. He wouldn't hurt a flea. He has a heart of gold. If you ask me, you're dead wrong about those boys."

"Mrs. Hoover," barked Mrs. Goodbody, "I did not ask you. Just get the files. Now!"

I peeked around the edge of the office door. Mrs. Goodbody had her back to me. Mrs. Hoover was digging through a filing cabinet. Her cheeks were red and she looked angrier than I had ever seen her look.

Mrs. Hoover, I thought, *I'm getting you a nice Christmas present this year.*

I tiptoed past the door and ran to the first display case. The kindergartners and first graders had almost filled them with lists in their jagged handwriting. I read one:

Ten things I like about our school:
1. lunch
2. recess
3. story time
4. snack
5. recess

6. my pencil
7. my eraser
8. share time
9. the tadpoles
10. going home

Yep, that just about summed it up. I moved on to the last case where there was room for our lists. I quickly tacked the first list to the corkboard backing of the case. I didn't want to be in the hall when Goodbody left for the day.

My list was stupid. I had actually tried to think of things I liked. It wasn't easy, but I did think of a couple of things. Mrs. Trump always played music in class. And every day, she wrote a quote on the chalkboard. She said she did it to inspire us.

Sometimes the quote was like reading a confusing fortune cookie. But sometimes, it really made sense. One of my favorites was *"Carpe diem."* It means "Seize the day." I wished I could do that, *seize the day*. I even wrote it on the front of my notebook.

The rest of my list was just food I liked in the cafeteria. I made up the last three. No way did our cafeteria serve iced mocha, tacos, or cinnamon rolls. But I figured Mrs. Goodbody didn't know that yet.

Most of the kids in my class had made ridiculous lists.

Mac's was my favorite:

1. burping
(oops I forgot that's not allowed)
2. hamsters in the classroom
(oops I forgot that's not allowed)
3. fire drills (are they still allowed?)
4. Mrs. Trump
(because she puts up with us)
5. football (oops I forgot that's not allowed)
6. running
(oops I forgot that's not allowed)
7. having a creative thought
(oops I forgot that's not allowed)
8. breathing (I guess that's still allowed)
9. my friends (Hey, Lido!)
10. I can't think of anything else
(which is probably not allowed)

I tacked up the last list and ran back to Mrs. Trump's class to put the tacks back. Mrs. Trump had gone home, but there was a big envelope on her desk. Across the front was printed "Putnam County School District, Retirement Benefits Enclosed."

"Mrs. Trump," I said to myself, "you can't leave us now."

Chapter Seven

Wednesday: Welcome to the Goodbody Grill

I tried to call Mac and tell him about our files and Mrs. Goodbody, but he wasn't home. His mom said, "He went to the library to do his homework." *Yeah, and I'm a three-headed giraffe*, I wanted to tell her, but I didn't.

My mom wouldn't let me go to the library. She said Mac and I would drive the librarian crazy. But we couldn't help it. When Mac and I went to the library, we practiced lip reading. Well, not *real* lip reading, just trying to guess what the other one was saying. We did it in Mrs. Trump's class sometimes when we got bored.

It always started out fine, but then one of us would get the other one wrong. Like maybe Mac would mouth "Do you have an eraser?" and I would think he said "Do you have Anna Racer?" Then we would start laughing. And then the librarian would tap us on the back and point to the door.

So I had to wait until Wednesday morning to talk to Mac. But on Wednesday, things got really weird.

The first thing I saw when I got to school was a crowd of kids standing around someone. That someone was Mac. He was standing near the edge of the street in front of the school steps. And he was putting on a show.

I could hear him long before I got there. It sounded like he was burping the theme to *Star Wars*.

"And now," Mac said when he was finished, "I think it's time for some action. Who has a math book they don't need?" A sea of hands held up their books. Mac picked one.

"Watch this." Mac started swallowing. And swallowing. He held the book slightly over his head, pointed toward the school. Then he burped right on it. The book shot up into the air in a beautiful arc, coming to rest on the roof. Right above the front doors of the school.

A cheer went up from our little circle. But then the front doors of the school flew open. It was Goodbody. And she looked mad.

"Mr. McGerp," she said, "I thought I made it clear that burping was not allowed on school property. Your parents will be hearing from me."

"Excuse me, Mrs. Goodbody," Mac said, "but last night I went to the library and looked at a map of the school's property. Actually, it ends right here." He took his toes and drew a line along the edge of the sidewalk. "Technically, the ground I'm on belongs to the county." He smiled.

Maybe he will be a lawyer, I thought.

Mrs. Goodbody looked like she really wanted to scream at Mac. If she could have shot death rays from her eyeballs, Mac would have been a piece of fried bacon.

But she saw all those kids staring at her. And she saw parents dropping off their kids. So she stopped herself. She took a big sip of air and smiled even though her eyes looked like two geysers ready to pop.

"We'll see, Mac McGerp," she said. "We'll see."

She turned and stormed back into the school.

"McGerp one, Goodbody zip," Mac said, grinning.

At morning assembly Mrs. Goodbody announced a new school dress code. She read from her clipboard. White shirts and black, gray, or navy blue pants. Red sweaters and sweatshirts only. No exceptions. "Starting tomorrow," she snapped.

Mac looked up from the map of the Bahamas that was spread across his lap. "No way!" he whispered.

"And one other thing," Mrs. Goodbody continued. "I am having the playground equipment removed next weekend. The equipment is old and hazardous. I am replacing it with a green foam pad. It is much safer and doesn't require watering like grass does."

We knew better than to groan. We just sat there quietly. I felt sorry for the little kids. They wouldn't get a chance to swing, or climb the tire structure, or slide into the sand pit.

"She can't do that," Mac whispered.

"I bet she can," I whispered back. "I think a principal can do anything she wants, pretty much."

"But that's like she's a dictator," said Mac.

"Yep," I said. "That's about it."

Mrs. Goodbody looked out at us with her beady little bird eyes. She smiled and said, "And now I have a special treat for Mrs. Trump's room."

My heart went up into my throat. I tried to swallow it down again, but it was stuck there, like a big piece of unripe nectarine.

"Today," she said, "I will be teaching her class. Mrs. Trump is home ill." She looked right at Mac. "I imagine it will be a very interesting day."

"Good move, Goodbody," Mac whispered. He folded the map and stuffed it into his back pocket.

We walked quietly to our homeroom. I could hear the "click, click, click" of Mrs. Goodbody's heels against the linoleum. We filed into class and sat down.

Mrs. Goodbody stood at the front of the class. The last person into the room was Henry Debois.

"You!" Mrs. Goodbody pointed to Henry. He dropped his backpack and froze, halfway to sitting down.

"Y . . . y . . . yes?" Henry quivered.

"You're first," Mrs. Goodbody said. She whacked the top of her desk with a ruler. "Come here!"

Poor Henry stumbled to the front of the room. I'd known Henry since kindergarten. He was no match for someone like Goodbody. He stood in front of her. I thought I could feel him shaking all the way to the back of the room.

"What is your name?" she said. Tap, tap, tap went the ruler on the desk.

"Uh, Henry," Henry whispered.

"Well, Henry," Mrs. Goodbody said. "Let's see what you know. And stop standing there like some hunchbacked cow. Stand up straight and answer clearly."

Then she grilled Henry on everything from colonial America to multiplying fractions. She threw in a couple of really hard spelling words for good measure. The whole time she wore a sneer on her face. A sort of you-dumb-little-rabbit,-I'm-going-to-eat-you-for-dinner look.

And poor Henry. He tried to answer each question fired at him. He held onto the bottom of his zip-up sweatshirt as if it were a life raft.

"Who was the third president of the United States?"

"Um. Um." Henry's hands were shaking. He chewed on his lower lip.

"You're taking far too long to answer," Mrs. Goodbody said. "You aren't terribly bright, are you, Henry?"

"I'm sorry," mumbled Henry.

"Sorry won't get you into college," she snapped. "Sorry won't help you make something of your miserable life."

Goodbody kept asking questions. I looked at the clock. She had been grilling Henry for ten minutes. I couldn't watch anymore. I looked over at Mac.

Mac was turning the funny green color he got when he held his burps. But it was his expression that shocked me. He had a look on his face that I had never seen before. He was looking at Goodbody. And it was a look of pure hatred.

Henry survived his drill with Goodbody and ran back to his seat. He put his head down on his desk, and although I didn't turn around to check, and I couldn't hear a sound, I bet he was crying.

Goodbody picked another victim. Then another. Her questions got harder. And faster.

Even Audrey Troll cracked, and Audrey had gotten an A on everything since I had known her. Goodbody just made it impossible to win her little game.

Audrey looked close to tears when she walked back to her desk. I figured it was the first time she hadn't done really well at something. Her lip quivered a little as she sat down.

Mac leaned over to her desk and whispered, "It's okay, Audrey. If she'd given you enough time to answer, you'd have gotten them all right."

Audrey beamed. It was the most Mac had ever said to her.

I looked up at the clock and realized it was almost time for the lunch bell. Part of me was glad, because I wanted out of that room. But part of me knew that because I hadn't been called yet, I was going to be tortured after lunch.

"Mac," I whispered, pointing at the clock. He gave me a thumbs-up. I smiled back.

Then Mrs. Goodbody said, "I need a special helper for the rest of the day. This helper will be having lunch with me." She walked up and down the aisles. "Who will the lucky student be?"

Not me not me not me, I chanted in my head. I couldn't think of anything worse than eating lunch with HER.

Click. Click. Click. Then she stopped. Right in front of Mac's desk.

"Mr. McGerp," she said, "you will be my helper today."

"Great," said Mac. "Does this mean you'll buy my lunch?"

The class twittered until Goodbody turned around and faced us. That shut us up.

"No, Mr. McGerp," she said. "But it does mean that you'll be with me for the rest of the day. No sneaking off for any reason. No recess. Just you and me. Is that clear?"

I looked at Mac. He was very green now. I just hoped he could make it to the end of the day.

Chapter Eight

Chicken Surprise Slide

I got in the line to buy lunch, right behind Audrey Troll.

"Is Mac okay?" she said.

"I sure hope so," I said. "He was looking like a ripe avocado before lunch."

"He was not!" Audrey punched me in the arm.

"Jeez. Take it easy," I said, rubbing my arm. "Remember me? I'm Mac's friend. I meant he was *really* looking green. He needs to burp."

"Oh, I'm sorry," said Audrey as she put a dish of Jell-O on her tray. She looked at me nervously. "You know, I don't like to say bad things about people. I believe that gossip is the sign of an uneducated mind."

She's going into brainiac mode, I thought.

"But . . ." She leaned over and whispered to me. "I really, really don't like Mrs. Goodbody."

"You mean you hate her," I said as I tried to make up my mind between the Chicken Surprise and the Weenie Rolls.

Audrey blushed. "I don't like that word," she said. "I prefer to say I really, really don't like her."

"Have it your way," I said. "Hate works for me, though."

Audrey had just finished paying for her lunch when Mrs. Goodbody came into the cafeteria. Mac was right behind her, greener than ever.

Goodbody was marching to the teachers' table. She carried a black bag that must have held her lunch. Mac was walking behind her. She couldn't tell, but he was imitating her walk. There was a lot of giggling, and a few kids laughed out loud.

"Isn't he wonderful?" gushed Audrey.

I couldn't help but admire her in a way. She didn't care who knew she was in love with Mac.

"Yeah, he's pretty cool, Audrey," I said.

Mrs. Goodbody slowed down. She must have suspected Mac was up to something, because she stopped and swung around to catch him at it. But her big black bag swung around, too, and it knocked the tray out of Randy Lubbock's hands.

His food went everywhere. Most of it landed right in front of Goodbody. A large yellow portion went on top of her black shoes. I think it was vanilla pudding, but at our school you can never tell.

Goodbody's face went bright red.

"Uh oh," I said. "This can't be good."

She turned and got very close to Randy. She shot a quick glance at the teachers' table.

"You half-wit!" she hissed quietly. "Look at what you've done to my shoes!" She looked Randy up and down. "You are an idiot." She leaned closer. "And a *pig*! What makes you think you should eat dessert? You have enough fat stored on that ugly preteen body of yours to survive all winter!"

Randy looked horrified. He looked down at his waist. I think he was trying to suck in his stomach.

"I'm sorry," he mumbled.

"Sorry!" Goodbody glared at us. "This is the sorriest group of students I have ever known!" She was starting to yell again. She stopped. She leaned over to Randy. "Clean it up," she hissed. "Now."

Goodbody whirled around and headed toward the teachers' bathroom—to clean up, I guess. But Mac's foot got in the way. Goodbody tripped and went face first into the pool of Randy's Chicken

Surprise that was oozing across the white floor tiles.

I looked up at the cafeteria lady. "I think I'll have the Weenie Rolls," I said.

Goodbody sputtered. She wiped Chicken Surprise off her face and flung it across the room. Some landed on the cafeteria lady's shirt. Goodbody stomped her feet. She started screeching. She yelled stuff at us we couldn't really understand. Maybe it was better that way.

It came out sort of like, "You hideous," sputter, gurgle, "fiends," sputter, "throttle," screech, "undeserving," choke, "brilliant career," sputter, "morons," babble, sputter.

We just stood there and watched her.

Finally, she stormed off to the teachers' bathroom. Mac sat down at our table. I gave him half a Weenie Roll. Audrey gave him her dessert.

"Did she see you trip her?" I whispered to him.

"I didn't trip her," Mac said as he swallowed his Jell-O. "I just had my foot there. She fell over it. I didn't do a thing."

Here we go again, I thought. "Well, you'd better hope she didn't *see* your foot anyway," I said.

I guess Goodbody didn't. She came out of the bathroom and sat down at the teachers' table. It seemed to me that all of the teachers started eating faster.

Goodbody saw Mac sitting with me and pointed at the chair across from her.

"Nice knowing you," I said.

"I'll live," Mac grinned.

I hoped so. I was pretty sure all the rumors about Goodbody were just rumors. I looked down at my Weenie Roll. I picked it up and inspected it.

Well, I don't think anyone is missing yet, I thought as I took a bite.

Chapter Nine

What Goes Up Must Come Down

After lunch, we reluctantly went back to class. I survived Goodbody's grilling. Mac seemed to enjoy his turn, although holding in his burps made his voice sound funny. I guess he didn't want to open his mouth very wide.

Mac made it to the 2:30 bell without burping. He almost mowed me down running out of the school.

"Get out of the way!" he screamed as he headed for the school parking lot.

I was right behind him. "He's gonna blow!" I

yelled. "Run for it!"

Kids scattered to the right and left of Mac. He ran to the end of the parking lot and then stopped short. He grabbed his stomach.

"Oh, no," he said.

"Mac?" I said. "Are you all right?"

"It's gonna be a big one!" he squeaked. "Get out of here, Lido!"

I ran behind the maintenance shed that bordered the parking lot. I peeked around the corner and saw Mac, standing alone.

"The coast is clear, Mac!" I yelled. I hoped Mrs. Goodbody was on the other side of the school. *Way* on the other side.

Then it happened.

To say Mac burped wouldn't do it justice. Mac erupted like a ten-year-old volcano of gas. The blast from Mac's parking lot burp will never be forgotten by those of us who witnessed it.

It left Mac and traveled along the length of the parking lot, away from the school. Luckily, there weren't any cars parked at that far end. Well, actually there was one. A big, black, beat-up old station wagon.

The blast cut down the row of trees that flanked the parking lot like a giant weed whacker. Snap. Snap. Snap. They went down like a tree domino line.

Dirt and small rocks from the parking lot swirled around above the blast. It looked like a tornado traveling right toward that ugly station wagon.

Then it hit it. That tornado burp scooped up the station wagon like a feather lying on the ground. Scooped it up and twirled it around and around in the sky. We came out from our hiding places to see better.

The sun glinted off the black paint as it spun around. It was truly a beautiful sight to behold. I wondered how long it would stay up there. I hoped forever. I ran over to Mac and put my arm on his shoulder.

"Look at that," Mac said. He sounded kind of dazed.

"It's amazing," I said. The wagon whirled in that burp tornado for the longest time. But finally, it started to slow down. And sink.

"Look out!" Mac screamed.

"Oh man oh man oh man!" I chanted.

The station wagon took a nosedive. I saw the sun flash off the glass of its headlights as it started down. I closed my eyes. CRASH! It hit in the middle of the street. Nose first. Right into the construction hole Mrs. Trump had warned us about.

"Uh oh," said Mac. "That car is toast."

"Yeah," I said. "You're lucky it was just a piece of

junk. Probably no one even owned it. Someone just left it in the parking lot. Like trash."

"Uh, Lido," Mac said. "I don't think so."

He pointed up to the trunk of the car. Dangling from the end was the license plate.

It said

GOODBDY

"Run," I said.

"Run fast," Mac said.

We ran all the way to my front yard.

"I'm so dead," Mac said. "She'll call my parents for sure."

"Maybe she'll think her brakes were broken. My uncle Rick forgot to set the emergency brake once, and his car ended up in the Weederton Putt Putt Golf Course. Backed right over the sphinx. Took its head right off."

"Lido, her car isn't just sitting in a hole. It's stuck straight up and down! It looks like some kind of fat, dented flagpole. Leaving your brake off wouldn't put you in a hole like that. No, she'll know who did it." He let out a deep sigh. "Now I'll never make it to the Bahamas."

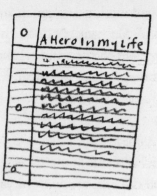

Chapter Ten

Thursday:
The Hero of Plunger Field

On Wednesday night my mom wanted to go out to dinner. And just to make sure I was really miserable, she made me get a haircut. I didn't get a chance to call Mac.

The next morning my mom overslept. I was late, so I ran as fast as I could to school. I wanted to see if Goodbody's car was still stuck in that hole. But it was gone. It was as if it had never happened.

There was a lot of whispering going on at morning assembly. A bunch of kids had seen Mac send that car up into the sky. Goodbody had to know it was him.

I looked at the empty space next to me on the bench. She must have called his parents. He was probably on his way to a private school in Siberia right now. School without Mac was going to be pretty boring. I felt a wave of sadness wash over me. I sure was going to miss him.

Someone slapped my back.

"Hey, Lido," Mac said. "How's life in the fast lane?"

"Mac!" I was so happy to see him I almost hugged him. "I thought you were gone for sure! Didn't Goodbody call your folks?"

"It's so weird," Mac said as he plopped down next to me. "She didn't call. I went back to school after dinner. A tow truck was there, hauling her car out of the hole. But she wasn't there. No . . ." He stared at the stage as though he were in a trance. "No, she's got some kind of plan for revenge. Getting rid of me isn't good enough."

"Mac," I said, "I know one thing. I wouldn't be you for anything."

Mac laughed. "What's the worst she can do? It's not like she's going to actually kill me. You don't believe that stuff about her, do you?" He looked back up at the stage. I thought he looked just a little worried. "I mean, I'm *pretty* sure some-one just made that stuff up." He shook his head. "Nah, the worst thing that can happen to me is that my folks will ship me off somewhere."

It was creepy. Goodbody didn't mention the fly-ing car at morning assembly. And nobody told on Mac. She didn't call Mac into her office. She just ignored him.

One good thing did happen, though: Mrs. Trump came back. She had a bad cold and it was hard for her to talk, so we did lots of reading and writing. She had us write an essay called "A Hero in My Life." I don't know any official heroes. But Mac did something once that saved Plunger's life. So I wrote about that.

I called it "Dog's Best Friend," and I thought it wasn't half bad. It went like this:

It was a hot summer afternoon when my hero, Mac McGerp, did his good deed. We were playing Burpball in the field in back of Mac's house. It was Mac, me, and Jarvis Pryor.

Burpball is kind of like soccer, only the goalie burps. He burps back any balls that get near him. Of course, Mac is always the goalie. It's pretty hard to score against Mac.

We played only one game that day, because it was so

hot. Then we sat under a tree to cool off.

"What's that sound?" Mac said to us.

"I don't hear nothing," said Jarvis Pryor.

"I don't either," I said.

We got quiet and then we could hear it, too. Something was whimpering. Maybe it was a little kid. Or a dog.

Mac walked across the field. "Hey, guys!" he said. "Come here!"

He was standing by an old drainage pipe about fifteen feet long and a foot wide.

"Something's stuck in there," Mac said.

We got down on our knees and looked in the pipe. I couldn't see a thing.

Mac ran back to his house and got a flashlight. He shined it in the pipe. We could see an animal's eyes peering back at us.

"Poor little thing," said Mac. "He's stuck. We've got to get him out."

"We can lift this thing up," said Jarvis. "This ain't no big deal." But we couldn't. It was a lot heavier than it looked. The whimpering was getting softer.

"Mac," I said. "What should we do?" I don't like emergencies. They make me nervous.

"Lido," Mac said, "get at the other end. I'm going to burp him out."

So I sat at the end of the pipe, arms out and ready to

catch whatever little creature was stuck inside. Mac started swallowing. And swallowing. I hoped he didn't burp
the pipe into a million pieces.

Then he stuck his face into the pipe and burped. Next
thing I knew, a furry ball was launched at my stomach.

"That thing is disgusting," said Jarvis, pointing at
the fur ball.

The little ball was a dog. At first I thought he was
dead. But Mac rubbed his back and talked to him. Pretty
soon, his tail was wagging. Then he was jumping up on
Mac and licking his face.

We took him back to Mac's house. Mac cleaned him
up and gave him something to eat. We found out that he
belonged to Mrs. Shropshire on Elm Street. She called
him Sweetie. We took him home to her. But Sweetie kept
running away to Mac's house.

Finally, Mrs. Shropshire just gave Sweetie to Mac.
She said Sweetie had picked who he wanted to live with.

Mac named him Plunger. He's been Mac's dog ever
since. Mac named the field in back of his house after him.
Plunger Field. It's where we play all our Burpball games.

And that's why Mac McGerp is a hero in my life.

The End

Not too bad, right? Anyway, the rest of the day
was pretty boring. Mrs. Trump didn't really feel well

enough to teach us. But don't get me wrong, I was very glad she was back.

Actually, one other thing did happen. Mr. Morgan, the superintendent of schools, made a surprise visit.

Chapter Eleven

Goodbody Goes to Kindergarten

Our class was lined up in the hall, waiting to go into the health room to watch a film.

"What's it about?" Mac asked me as we leaned against the wall.

"I'm not sure, but Mrs. Trump told me she thinks it's called 'Hygiene Is Your Friend.'"

That's when the double doors at the end of the hall swung open. A man wearing a gray striped suit marched through them. He reminded me of Mac's dad. Mr. Business. He walked like he was pretty important. And he was headed in our direction.

"Who's that?" I said.

Mac shrugged his shoulders.

The man came over to Mrs. Trump.

"Good afternoon," he said. "I'm Mr. Morgan, superintendent of schools. And you are . . . ?"

"Mrs. Trump," she said.

"And these fine young people." He looked up and down our line. "They are your students?"

"Yes, Mr. Morgan," Mrs. Trump said. "This is my fifth-grade class."

"Well," he said. "Don't mind me. Pretend I'm not here. I just want to observe your class. I like to drop in now and then and see what's new."

The door to the health room opened. Mrs. Cook, the health teacher, waved us in. Just as we were about to file in and take our seats, Mrs. Goodbody swished toward our little group.

"Oh, Superintendent Morgan," she gushed. "I saw you from my office door. What an honor to have you here at Walters Elementary." She smoothed down her dress. "I had no idea you were coming here today."

"That's the general idea, Mrs. Goodbody," he said. "I like to come and observe the schools that are having a little trouble." He looked her in the eye. "Just to make sure everything is going well."

"I can assure you that the children and I are getting along *famously*," Mrs. Goodbody said in a syrupy voice. "We've been working on getting organized, haven't we children?" She put her arm around Audrey.

Now, there were thirty-two kids in Mrs. Trump's class. And I'm sure there were thirty-two kids with their mouths open in complete and utter disbelief. Poor Audrey just looked like a piece of petrified wood.

I looked at Mac.

Uh oh, I thought. Mac looked as if he were about to say something. Then he did.

"Actually, Mr. Morgan," Mac said, "I don't think things are going well at all."

I cringed. What was he doing now?

"I believe," Mac said, "that some of our civil liberties have been crushed." He smiled up at Mr. Morgan. "And our educational opportunities are being limited."

I was afraid to look at Mrs. Goodbody.

"Is that so?" said Mr. Morgan. "Well, you seem to be a well-spoken young man. What's your name?"

"Mac McGerp," he said.

"*The* Mac McGerp?" asked Mr. Morgan. "Well, now." He slapped Mac on the back. "Ready for the

Nationals, son? Withersberg is counting on you."

Mac smiled. "Yes, sir."

Mr. Morgan looked at Mrs. Goodbody. "What's this about crushing civil liberties?"

I looked at Mrs. Goodbody. She had a weird smile on her face. She launched an attempt at damage control.

"Oh, Mac," Mrs. Goodbody said, laughing, I mean, I guess you could call it a laugh. It sounded sort of like gargling. "Mac has such a vivid imagination," she sighed. She let go of Audrey and walked over to Mac. "He's a very bright boy." She put her arm around Mac. Around *Mac*! Can you believe it? "Sometimes he lets his imagination get the best of him."

Mac reached up and took her arm off his shoulder. Mrs. Goodbody tensed. She grabbed Mr. Morgan firmly by the arm and whirled him in the other direction.

"Let me show you our lists, Mr. Morgan," she said. She practically shoved him down the hall. "And we have a lovely new banner I want you to see. Besides, I'm sure you've seen your share of health films."

Mr. Morgan looked over his shoulder at Mac. "I'll speak to you about this matter later," he said.

Mrs. Trump herded us into the health room.

Mac hummed. He had that look he got when he was proud of himself. Me? I was just happy Goodbody had left. It could have gotten ugly.

Mac and I practiced lip reading through the movie. I mean, seriously, who cares about Ted Tooth Decay and Arthur Armpit Odor? Like we didn't have mothers and fathers yelling at us to take showers and brush our teeth every five minutes.

Anyway, after the film, we started walking back to Mrs. Trump's class. She stopped. She turned to me and Mac.

"I've left my set of keys on Mrs. Cook's desk. Would you two run down and get them for me, please?"

Mac and I jogged down the hall. Mrs. Cook wasn't in the room. I walked over to the desk and got Mrs. Trump's keys. Mac was smiling.

"What are you so happy about?" I asked.

"Lots of things. I struck a blow for our rights, for one thing," he said. "And Mr. Morgan wants to talk to me." He closed Mrs. Cook's door behind us. We started walking back to Mrs. Trump's room. "And I'm getting better at holding my burps. I can go until two-thirty, no problem. Maybe even three-fifteen."

I dropped the keys. When I turned around to pick them up, I saw Goodbody. She was outside Mrs. Cook's door, standing there with her scrawny arms crossed over her chest. Had she been listening to us? I couldn't tell. But she looked very satisfied about something.

Mrs. Goodbody kept Mr. Morgan pretty busy. She took him to every class in the school. And she made sure he didn't get anywhere near Mac. The last time I saw him was when I was turning in the attendance report to the office for Mrs. Trump.

They were in the kindergarten room. Mr. Morgan was surrounded by a sea of five-year-olds. Mrs. Goodbody was singing "Old MacDonald" with them. She tried to act as if she did it every day. But the kindergartners knew better. They sat close to their teacher, or by Mr. Morgan. When Mrs. Goodbody did an "oink oink here and an oink oink there," she was sitting on the carpet all by herself.

Right before the bell to go home rang, Mrs. Trump reminded us one more time about the Science Fair.

"And don't forget," she said. "Mr. Morgan, our school superintendent, will be there. Let's show him how much we know about science."

I looked over at Mac. He was smiling again.

After school that day, Mac and I decided that Plunger Field was a good place for him to burp.

Nothing to break. No cars, no people. Just a field with weeds and a few bushes here and there.

Mac and I ran all the way there. Mac burped a big one. Luckily, he just sent dust and grass flying. No one got hurt. It did leave a path across the field, as if someone had driven a giant lawn mower straight out in front of us.

Mac lay down and rubbed his stomach. I sat down next to him.

"You know," I said. "It's just weird that Goodbody hasn't mentioned her car. Or done anything about the sign on her butt. She's up to something. You should get sick for a couple of days, Mac."

"Can't," Mac said. "Tomorrow is the Science Fair, remember? My dad's been working on my science project like crazy. It would trash him if I didn't get to display it."

"Yeah," I said. "My mom's been working pretty hard on mine, too. What's yours going to be?"

"A replica of the gastrointestinal tract. It's pretty cool. You should see what happens after you put the food in. Very gross. What's yours?"

"A working model of a head louse," I said. "My mom even made a human scalp for it to suck on. She used some old wig she found at a thrift store. She's pretty proud of it."

We walked to his house. Plunger came bounding down the back steps.

"Well, I guess we'll just have to wait and see what she's up to," Mac said.

"Guess so," I said, patting Plunger's head. "But I don't like it."

Chapter Twelve

Friday: Trapped Like Rats

Friday morning I woke up early so I could draw a new surfboard design I'd dreamt about. I wanted to show it to Mac. Maybe we could use it on one of our boards when we opened the Surf & Burp. When I finished, I got dressed and packed my lunch. I packed extra because I'd promised Mrs. Trump that I'd watch the science projects until the Science Fair started at 6:30. With Mac.

Oh, no, I thought. *That's why Goodbody didn't do anything about her car. She's got me and Mac until 6:30 tonight. Mac will never be able to hold his burp that long.*

I've got to call him!

I ran into the kitchen and grabbed the phone.

"Excuse me, young man," my mom said. She was sitting at the table, trying to wake up. "Just *who* do you think you're calling at seven in the morning?"

"I have to call Mac," I said. "It's an emergency!"

"Exactly what kind of an emergency?" she asked, stirring her coffee.

"If Mac goes to school today, he'll have to spend the whole day with Goodbody, and if he does, he won't get to burp and then something terrible will happen!"

She sipped her coffee and gave me her Lido,-you're-a-little-nuts look. "It can wait until seven-thirty," she said.

"But Mom," I said.

"No buts," she said.

I got my backpack and sat at the table. I watched the clock. Each minute lasted about three hours. Finally it was 7:30.

I called. It rang and rang. No answer.

"Now he's not home!" I said. "You should have let me call!"

"Lido," she said as she rubbed her temples, "watch that tone with your mother."

I grabbed my backpack and ran out the door.

I ran all the way to Mac's house. Plunger was happy to see me. He jumped up and down next to me as I raced up the walk. I pounded on the door. No one answered. The car wasn't in the driveway.

I stood there for a minute and caught my breath. It wasn't going to be a good day at school, that much I knew. I wanted to go home, get back in bed, and hide. But I knew I couldn't. Mac was my friend. I had to help him.

"And besides, what am I, anyway? A man . . . or a mouse?" I said to Plunger. I scratched his ears. Then I took off for school.

I got there late because I creamed myself by tripping over a branch that got caught on my shoe. It took me a minute to brush off and get going again. By the time I reached the school doors, the 8:00 bell had already rung.

Maybe he went somewhere else today, I thought as I tried to sneak into the auditorium. Mrs. Goodbody was going on and on about the Science Fair. I looked around for Mac and couldn't see him. I started to breathe more easily. *Ha!* I thought. *She can't get him now!*

But I was wrong. Because when I looked up on the stage, there he was, sitting in a chair next to Mrs. Goodbody.

Mrs. Goodbody said, "And you can see that I

have one of my special helpers here today. I'm still waiting for my other helper, Lido Katz. Is Mr. Katz out there?"

Jarvis Pryor shoved me into the aisle.

"Thanks a lot, Jarvis," I growled.

"No problem," he giggled.

"Oh, I see Mr. Katz has decided to come to school after all," Mrs. Goodbody said. "Would you please join us up here on the stage?"

I walked carefully up the steps. All I needed was to trip in front of the whole school. I sat down next to Mac. He didn't look so good to me. I tried to smile at him, but Goodbody was glaring at me, so I didn't.

"Now that my helpers are here," she said, "let's have them help, shall we? Mr. Katz, Mr. McGerp, come up to the microphone. Mr. Katz, you'll say the Pledge of Allegiance. Mr. McGerp, you'll sing the national anthem. The rest of you will stand at attention and listen."

Me? Say the pledge all by myself? In front of everybody? I felt my knees go a little squishy.

I looked at Mac. How was he going to sing that song without burping? He loved to burp that song. He'd won seven trophies for burping the national anthem.

"Mr. Katz." She held on to the z in my last name.

"We are waiting."

"Okay," I said. I could hear my heartbeat drumming in my ears. The pledge. How did that go again? Oh yeah.

"I pledge allegiance to the flag . . ." No one laughed when I was finished, so I guess I did all right.

"Now, Mr. McGerp." She smiled. I got those goose bumps on my arms again.

Mac started to sing, "Oh, say can you see . . ." His voice sounded weird. I knew he was trying really hard not to burp. The last thing he needed was to get suspended on the day of the Science Fair.

". . . and the home of the brave." Mac closed his lips tight. Beads of sweat were on his forehead.

Mrs. Goodbody looked disappointed.

She turned back to her microphone and said, "You may now go to class."

Some of the teachers came up to Goodbody to talk. I leaned over to Mac.

"Are you okay?" I asked.

"Yeah," he said. "But I almost lost it a couple of times. Those high notes were killer."

"Mac, we have to be here until six-thirty!" I whispered. "With Goodbody!"

Mac had forgotten. I could tell by the shocked look on his face.

"What am I going to do?" he asked.

Suddenly, Goodbody's thin face was thrust between us. "What you are going to do," she smirked, "is stay with me all day. I told you I'd think of a punishment for your little prank."

Mac and I looked at each other. We were cooked.

Clawing your Way to the Top

How to Eliminate Friends and Influence People That Really Matter

DISCIPLINE Through the Ages

Chapter Thirteen

Wild Beast on Campus!

It was the worst day of school ever. Spending the day with Mrs. Goodbody was as much fun as having a dentist drill your teeth.

She marched us into her office and closed the door behind her.

"The next time you think of writing poetry and sticking it on my backside," she said, "or blasting my car up into the air with one of your hideous burps, or trying to make trouble for me with the superintendent of schools, you'll think twice."

"But, Lido had nothing to do with any of that,"

said Mac.

She whipped her head around and looked at me. "Then maybe he should start picking his friends a little more carefully."

She made us sit in chairs, one on each side of her desk.

"Let's start with the discipline of silence. I don't want to hear one word from either of you. I need to read my mail."

I glanced at the top of her desk. She had a stack of books next to the rat's cage. One was *How to Eliminate Friends and Influence the People that Really Matter.* Another one was *Clawing Your Way to the Top in Five Easy Lessons.*

Goodbody picked up a letter opener. It was silver with a black handle and looked more like a knife. She stuck the sharp point into the corner of an envelope and ripped it open. I let out a sigh of relief.

I looked at her from the corner of my eye. She had on that black dress again. Or maybe she had dozens of them, lined up in her closet like bats in a cave. She made a disgusting little smacking noise with her lips when she read each piece of mail.

She smelled like the give-away clothes barrel at the YMCA—musty with a hint of old food and sweat. I tried breathing out of my mouth. It helped a little. I watched the rat for a while. I wondered if he knew what Goodbody had in store for him.

After she finished her mail, we had to walk around the campus after her. If she saw a piece of trash, it was, "Mr. McGerp, pick that up." If she saw a piece of gum stuck to the sidewalk it was, "Mr. Katz, scrape that off."

We still weren't allowed to talk. Just walk and sit behind her like two well-trained dogs. But Mac and I knew how to get around that. We did our lip reading.

While we tromped around after her, we talked. Once Mac mouthed, "Isn't she the ugliest goon on earth?" and I mouthed back, "She is an evil alien witch." The only problem was trying not to laugh.

After lunch, she made us clean the windows in the library. Goodbody loaded us down with window cleaner and rags. She sat at a table and read a book while we worked. I looked at the title. It was *Discipline Through the Ages*.

Cleaning the windows wasn't so bad, really. You got to look out the windows. That's how Mac and I saw Plunger. Sometimes Plunger followed Mac to school. Unfortunately, Goodbody saw him, too. She screamed for Mr. Henkley on the intercom.

Mr. Henkley rushed in.

"Stray dog, Mrs. Goodbody?" he asked. He wiped his hands on a cloth and stuck it in his back pocket.

"That repulsive beast over there!" She pointed out the window at Plunger. Plunger looked up at us and wagged his tail. Mr. Henkley tried not to smile.

"Call the pound!" she ordered. "We cannot have wild animals roaming our campus. A student could be bitten. Think of the lawsuits!"

"But Mrs. Goodbody," blurted Mac. "That's not a wild animal. That's my dog, Plunger. He wouldn't hurt anyone. He's even afraid of our cat!"

She turned and gave him an evil lizard stare. "I told you to be silent," she grunted. "You know the rules, Mr. McGerp. There are no animals allowed on this campus." She looked out the window with disgust. "That creature is going to the pound."

At least he isn't going to the cafeteria, I thought.

Mac and I looked at Mr. Henkley. And we both saw him do it. He winked and made an "okay" sign with his fingers. We knew Mr. Henkley wasn't going to send Plunger *anywhere*.

Mac grinned at him and mouthed, "Thank you."

Good old Mr. Henkley.

"You make the rules," Mac said to Mrs. Goodbody. He stood there like an angel.

"Don't get smart with me," she snapped at Mac. "Go get that dog!" she said to Mr. Henkley.

Mac and I watched through the window while Mr. Henkley picked Plunger up. He walked toward the toolshed by the back fence.

Mrs. Goodbody grunted with satisfaction.

Mac looked at me and grinned. I sprayed a happy face with the cleaner and wiped it away. We cleaned windows until 2:30. Mac wouldn't lip-read with me anymore. I knew it was because his burps were backing up. How was he going to make it until the Science Fair?

Chapter Fourteen

Volcanoes and Head Lice

After school, kids started dragging their science projects into the auditorium. Mac and I had to set up the tables. Then we had to organize the projects by grade.

Mac looked bad. "Maybe you should go home," I said.

He grabbed a sheet of paper and wrote, "No way. My parents canceled three meetings so they could come tonight."

"But you can't hold a burp that long," I said.

Mac shook his head. "I'm not going to burp," he

wrote. "I'm going to the Bahamas. And I'm going to talk to Mr. Morgan."

Oh man, I thought. *This was going to be rough.*

Mrs. Goodbody handed me a clipboard. She told me to write down the name of everyone who brought in a project.

"I want a hundred percent participation," she said. What was *I* supposed to do? Go over to some kid's house and make him do a thirty-minute science project? Get real. Still, I did make a note to myself to thank my mom for the head lice project.

At 4:00, Mrs. Goodbody took Mac with her. He looked horrible. Kind of a pasty gray, with a little red under the eyes. I smiled at him and gave him the thumbs-up. But he didn't give me one back. That worried me.

By 5:00, I was getting really nervous. I hadn't seen Mac for an hour. What if Jarvis was right? Maybe Goodbody was stuffing Mac into the cafeteria freezer behind the orange juice bars, right now!

Audrey Troll came in, carrying a volcano packed with baking soda and a bottle of vinegar.

"Audrey!" I yelled. "Just the person I want to see." I gave her the clipboard and told her that Goodbody would eat her and me if she screwed up.

"I don't want to do this," she said as she handed the clipboard back. "I need to set up my volcano.

It's very delicate."

"Let me put it this way," I said. "Mac *wants* you to do this. It would really help him."

"It would?" she gushed. "Okay." She grabbed the clipboard back. "I'll do it."

I had to check on Mac. Even if he wasn't in the freezer with the orange juice bars, he had *never* gone this long without burping before. Maybe I could distract Mrs. Goodbody somehow, just long enough for him to run out back and burp. I could think of something. After all, Mac was my friend and he needed me.

Chapter Fifteen

He Bloats

The school halls were mostly empty, except for the occasional kid, burdened by science, staggering toward the auditorium. I figured Mrs. Goodbody probably had Mac in her office. I crept along the hall until I got to her door.

It was quiet. But then I heard a little squeaking sound. Was that the rat? It squeaked again. Then I knew. That sound was Mac. That was the sound he made when he tried *not* to burp.

I crawled over to the office counter. I peeked around the end. There was Mac. He was sitting in a chair facing the window. Mrs. Goodbody was in front of Mac, with her back to him. She was looking out the window. I glanced at the clock. 5:15.

Squeak. He made that little anti-burp sound again.

Mrs. Goodbody cleared her throat. "You know, Mr. McGerp, I don't like children. So you can imagine how much I dislike children who burp."

Mac nodded his head and squeaked.

"A woman of my capabilities should be running a country. *Not* dealing with snot-nosed vermin like you." She looked at her fingernails for a minute. "And if you think you are going to stand in the way of me obtaining a position on the Board of Education, you are sadly mistaken."

She turned and faced Mac. I held my breath. She didn't see me. She put her hands on the arms of Mac's chair. "I think you need a lesson," she said. "And I'm going to give you one. You think you're special. You think that blowing gas out of your mouth makes you better than me? It certainly does not."

Mac squeaked something I couldn't hear.

"Do you think it is wise to be funny right now?" Mrs. Goodbody didn't like whatever it was Mac squeaked. "I don't think so." She looked up at the clock. "We have an hour and fifteen minutes until the Science Fair begins. When you do burp, and you *will*, you'll damage my office. Which is school property. Resulting in your immediate suspension."

She touched her forefinger to her lips. She pretended to look sad. "You won't get to compete in your ludicrous competition. Your parents won't be able to send you to St. Anne's. And best of all . . ." Now she was smiling. A big, wide happy smile. All of her teeth showed. It was disgusting. "You won't get a chance to talk to Mr. Morgan. And even if you do, once he finds out that you've broken a school rule *and* damaged school property, I'm sure he'll think twice about anything you *do* have to say."

She pulled a chair over to the window and sat down. "And if you *don't* burp . . . well, I don't think that's very likely. No, it's far more likely that you *will*. But if you don't, we'll just have to see what happens then, won't we?" She tapped on the arm of her chair. Tap. Tap. Tap.

"You'll thank me, you know," she said. "When you grow up and look back, you'll thank me."

Mac snorted.

"You still have an hour and ten minutes to go," she snapped. "Shut up and don't disturb me." She picked up some papers on her desk and started to read.

I just stayed crouched behind the counter,

watching the clock.

At 6:00 Mac started squirming in his seat. He'd never gone this long before. It seemed to me his whole body was puffing up. Maybe all those burps were causing him to bloat.

He turned his head to one side and saw me crouched behind the counter. I gasped. I couldn't help it. He looked so completely miserable. Tears were streaming down his face. I knew then that he wasn't going to burp. It wasn't just about getting to the National Burping Competition. Mac didn't want to give in to Goodbody.

That's when I got mad. Really mad. I mean, who was this Neanderthal to pick on him like this? And what kind of rat was I to just sit here and do nothing? It was time for action! *Carpe diem*! Seize the day! I stood up. I took a deep breath.

"Stop this right now!" I blurted out.

I clamped my hand over my mouth. Had that come from me? I saw Goodbody stiffen and turn slowly toward me. She looked white with anger. I felt my knees go weak.

"*What* did you say?" she hissed.

"Uh, uh," I stuttered.

Her eyes were drilling holes in my forehead. I considered my options. I could run out the door. Maybe Mac would follow me. I looked over at Mac.

He wasn't going anywhere. I could tell by his face. His jaw was set. Hard.

"Mr. Katz." Mrs. Goodbody took a step toward me. "*What* did you just say to me?"

I sighed and stood up as straight as I could with my wobbly knees.

"It's just that it's hurting him," I said. "Look at him!"

Goodbody looked at Mac.

"All he has to do is burp," she said. "Then he'll feel much better."

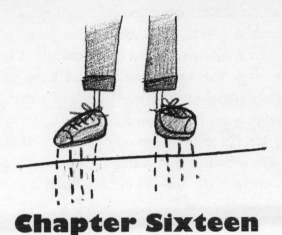

Chapter Sixteen

Time for 911?

"Sit down, Mr. Katz," she said. "You can watch the fun."

"Burp, Mac," I pleaded with him. "It's not worth this. We'll get to the Bahamas some other way."

"Yes, Mr. McGerp." Mrs. Goodbody's voice was thick and sticky like molasses. "By all means, do burp. Then I can be rid of you forever. I'm sure Mr. Morgan will be very interested in the police report on my car. All I need is to catch you in the act, just once. Maybe I can even get rid of your ridiculous little pip-squeak of a friend."

Pip-squeak? What the heck was that? I was just about to call her a wart-nosed hog-faced slimeball when Mac stood straight up from his chair.

Mac looked twice as big as normal. His sides were all puffed out. His neck was fat. Even his eyes were bugging out a little. He looked weird. Like some pool toy that was overinflated.

"Mac?" I said. But he didn't answer. He started shaking. First, his head started. Then his shoulders. His stomach. His hips. All the way down to his toes.

"Uh oh," I said to Mrs. Goodbody. "This can't be good. Do something!"

"Don't be stupid," Mrs. Goodbody growled. "He is just trying to get sympathy. Well, it won't work. I don't have any sympathy. Never had. Never will. So sit down!" She pointed at Mac. "And you sit down, too, you gaseous little wart!"

Goodbody was getting all worked up. I think seeing Mac like that was making her nervous. But Mac didn't sit down. He started bouncing.

Mac's feet went up and down about two inches off the floor. Bounce. Bounce. Bounce. He had a faraway look in his eyes.

"Mac?" I said. "Maybe I should call nine-one-one!" I said to Goodbody. I started toward the phone on her desk.

"I said sit down!" she screamed. She shoved me

down, hard, into a chair.

That's when it happened. Something about Goodbody shoving me snapped Mac back into the real world. He reached over and grabbed her arm.

"Stop it!" he yelled. And then he burped.

Chapter Seventeen

Goodbody's Ride

It was just like when you blow up a balloon and then let it go. Mac shot around that room. Backward, really, with all that gas shooting out his mouth. He'd go up one side and down another. You couldn't tell where he would go next. And all the time he was dragging Mrs. Goodbody along.

"Ha . . . ha . . . help!" she screeched as she grazed the top of the bookshelves. Books and papers went flying everywhere. I ducked behind her desk. Mac was like a human roller coaster. And Mrs. Goodbody was along for the ride.

The strange thing was, he didn't seem to be slowing down. I tried to see his face as he whirled by. Then I realized *why* he wasn't slowing down. He was swallowing more air while he was flying! He was reloading and reburping!

"Hey, Lido!" he burped. "Look at me (erp)! I'm flying!"

"Mac!" I yelled at him. "Stop burping! Are you crazy? You'll get suspended for sure!"

"I don't care!" he belched. "This (erp) is the most (erp) amazing thing (erp) I've ever done! I'm making (erp) history! I'm (erp) a flying human burp (erp)!"

He soared over the desk.

"I could do this forever (erp)! I just have to keep (erp) swallowing!"

"Mac! Stop!" I yelled up at him as he spun around the light fixture on the ceiling. Mrs. Goodbody's dress was like a sail in a windstorm. Sometimes it was flat against her sides. Sometimes it was up over her head.

"Ahhhhhh!" she screamed. Her mouth was a big *O*.

Mac whizzed by my head. It seemed like the reloading and reburping was making him go faster. Mrs. Goodbody's shoe hit me in the forehead as she zoomed by.

"Ouch!" I yelled. "Hey, that hurt! Slow down! Watch where you're dragging her!"

But then Mac started spinning even faster. Around and around and around. And Mrs. Goodbody suddenly flew off, just like when you play crack-the-whip. She flew headfirst into the small metal trash can next to her desk.

"Are you okay?" I yelled to her. She sat up with the trash can on her head. It was on there *tight*. I could see the outline of her nose poking through.

She swayed back and forth.

"Oooooooh," she said. "Oooooooh."

That can't be good, I thought.

Meanwhile, Mac was flying in tighter and tighter circles. Faster and faster. Then it happened. Mac flew straight up. Right through the roof.

Boom!

Mac was flying up to the clouds.

Chapter Eighteen

Up and Away

"Hang on, Mrs. Goodbody," I yelled at the trash can on her head. "I'll be right back! I have to get help for Mac! He's going into outer space!"

"Ooooooh. Eeeeeee," said Mrs. Goodbody.

"Yeah, that's right, Mrs. Goodbody!" I yelled. "Just stay right there!" And because she still had that trash can on her head, I did one thing before I ran for help. I reached over and opened the door to the rat's cage.

"Run for it, buddy," I whispered. I can't be sure, but it looked like that rat smiled at me. I gently touched his back to get him going. "*Carpe diem*," I told him. His whiskers twitched. Then he shot out of the cage, flew down the desk, and ran straight down the hall. He didn't look back once. I think he was a very smart rat.

I ran out of the office, too. I crashed through the doors to the parking lot. Everyone in the auditorium had filed out to see what the big boom was about. They were looking up at the sky.

I put my hand over my eyes to shield the sun. Mac was going higher and higher. I remembered the time I lost my helium balloon at the zoo. I had stood there and watched it turn into a tiny speck in the sky. Now I was watching my best friend do the same thing.

"What will they think of next," a parent next to me said, chuckling. "That's some science project. First time anyone has been allowed to launch a rocket."

"That's no science project," I said sadly. "That's Mac McGerp."

Chapter Nineteen

After the Big One

I was really sad. *Really* sad. Mac didn't come down from that burp. Mr. Bertram said it was too cold up there to survive. That or the fall did him in. The fire trucks and the ambulance showed up. But there was nothing they could do. Well, they did do one thing. They cut the trash can off Goodbody's head.

The whole town was sad. People wanted to put up a statue of Mac in the town square.

Audrey Troll couldn't stop crying. She carried a box of Kleenex everywhere she went. She sobbed all day, and probably all night, too. I didn't blame her. But you know what made me the saddest? That Mac and I would never get to open the Surf & Burp in the Bahamas. We were going to work side by side. It would have been perfect. That was all over now.

Superintendent Morgan fired Mrs. Goodbody that night at the Science Fair. I told him about Mac and how she said she would suspend him if he burped.

"Mrs. Goodbody," he growled, "I'm not sure what line of work you *should* be in, but children should not be a part of it."

"Mac said she should work in a prison," I told him sadly.

"Maybe," Mr. Morgan said. "Maybe."

Jarvis Pryor said Mr. Henkley escorted Mrs. Goodbody off the school grounds. She yelled a blue streak at him the whole way. I bet he was glad to see her gone. We all were.

Mrs. Trump was so upset over Mac that she decided to try to be the next principal at Walters.

"I couldn't possibly do as badly as *that* woman," she told me. "Besides, I've given it a lot of thought. I'm just not ready to retire. There are still students who need me." She ruffled my hair. "And I want to be there for them."

Good old Mrs. Trump. I hoped she got the job.

She'd be a really good principal.

Me? I couldn't even eat from being so sad about losing Mac. My best friend. Gone forever. All day Saturday and Sunday I just sat around. Monday they called off school in honor of Mac. I just lay on the couch.

Tuesday, Wednesday, and Thursday my mom let me stay home sick. "You've had quite a shock," she said. She knew how much Mac meant to me.

On Friday after school I walked over to Mac's house to pet Plunger. He was really glad to see me. I said hi to Mac's parents, too. They seemed really sad. They said it brought a little bit of Mac back just to see me.

They also said they were going to sue Mrs. Goodbody for not letting Mac burp. Something about free speech. I didn't understand all of what they said. They talk like lawyers a lot. Mrs. McGerp started crying when I told her I had to get going. They wanted me to come over again soon. Mac would have been surprised at how sad they were.

When I got home my mom was making dinner.

"Lido, could you bring in the mail?" she called.

"Sure," I sighed.

I trudged back to the mailbox. I reached in and pulled out a handful of mail. Grocery fliers. Bills. And a postcard. On the front was a picture of a beautiful beach with palm trees. At the bottom of the picture it said, "Sunset in the Bahamas." I flipped it over. It was addressed to me.

It said:

Hey, Lido!

What a ride! The landing was a little rough, (Big ouch!)
I sure hope they fired Goodbody.
Wish you were here.
This place is perfect.
Be home soon. I'm working on my take-offs & landings.

Miss you, buddy!
P.S. Could you let my folks know I'm okay?

It wasn't signed. There was just a happy face drawn at the bottom. But I knew that handwriting. It was Mac.

"Yes!" I yelled as I threw my fist high in the air. "Yes! Yes! Of course!"

Audrey Troll could put those tissues away!

I ran back to my front door. "Mom! I'll be right back!" I yelled in. "I heard from Mac!"

"You *what*?" she said. I could hear her yelling for me to come back and explain myself. But I was running as fast as I could to Mac's house. Because I had to let his folks know. Their pound puppy was just fine.

"Wahoo!" I yelled as I ran. "Mac is okay!" When I got to Mac's yard, I stood and looked at his house.

I felt the warm sun on my face and the cool wind blowing against my jacket. Life was good. Not just good . . . it was great. My best friend was alive. He was coming home. Goodbody was gone. Mac and I would walk to school together just like we always did.

Plunger bounded up the walk to greet me.

"Good news, boy," I said as I reached down to pet him. "The Surf and Burp is right on schedule."